The Clay of Vases
and Other Stories

By
Edgar John L'Heureux, Jr.

Copyright © 1987 by Edgar John L'Heureux Jr.

All rights reserved. For reproductions of this book of any kind or length, permission in writing must be received from Janus Press, P.O. Box 3633, Winter Springs, Fl 32708.

ISBN 0-9616341-1-1

Printed in the United States of America

First Edition
1 2 3 4 5 6 7 8 9 10

Printing by McNaughton & Gunn

TABLE OF CONTENTS

**THIS BOOK
IS DEDICATED TO**

My dad, Edgar John L'Heureux, Sr., for his loving assistance in my quest to write and market decent fiction, and to my son, Scott Bradford L'Heureux, for being such a good citizen growing up that I had time to write, not having to worry the slightest about his progress as a fine son.

ACKNOWLEDGMENT

Special thanks for this book is extended to Mr. Dennis Mullenix of Literary Services, Inc., Peoria, Illinois, for his tremendous assistance in making my work more meaningful to the reader.

And special thanks also to Joy Morse and Laura Noveck of Wordmasters, Orlando, Florida, for their typing expertise and their heartfelt encouragement of my writing endeavors.

Recognition and appreciation is expressed by the author to Mr. William Thomas of Ann Arbor, Michigan for his care and concern in making this book a reality.

THE CLAY OF VASES

The first day I met him I was clanking around with our lawnmover in the backyard a few weeks before my fourteenth birthday, wishing I were playing baseball with my buddies instead of mowing the lawn.

He had been hired by my father in April, during the slow season — that merciful pause before the hectic furniture moving binge of summer which engulfed the family business each year. That day, he was on a ladder painting wooden eaves and rafters on my father's furniture warehouse, a recently constructed, unadorned, one-story building adjacent to our modest frame house in a quiet residential neighborhood.

I had not noticed his presence as I clattered about, practically dragged along by the galloping Yazoo mower with its funny bicycle tires spinning like miniature Ferris wheels. From his perch with the paint bucket high atop the ladder, he acidly shot down a greeting with a devilish twinkle in his eye.

"You gonna fool around all day or really get some work done sometime soon?"

I mumbled an answer, not liking his salutation of introduction.

Hey, I thought irksomely, *he's a new man working for my father ... what does he know about how I work; and furthermore, what right does he have to slam me like that?*

This early encounter, however, etched vividly from my youth, did not set the tone for our relationship, which thereafter budded, blossomed, then flourished. It has long since been elevated to the lofty meadows of respect and admiration, enduring today, three decades later, beyond the poet's best description of friendship itself.

My mother and father operated a family moving-and-storage business for twenty-seven years in our sleepy neighborhood, at the edge of a college community, which was juxtaposed to the largest and best known Central Florida city. There, in that setting, in a leftover World War II, pre-fabricated frame house with adjoining business office, fitted together experimentally by my father with his two, eager and courageous hands, my sister and I sprouted from early childhood. Amid the loud, honest-sweat commotion of liveried trucks, loading and unloading household goods to and from the hodgepodge collection of furniture warehouses, which my dauntless father had also erected himself on our little plot of the planet, we grew to full adulthood.

Our drayman came to work that day, and stayed and stayed, touching all our lives with his presence for a generation and beyond. With his coming, and throughout his stalwart presence among us, our family business was never the same again. It became better because of him. He was the catalyst, the reagent, the pump-prime, the swizzle stick that stirred the proverbial drink.

Certainly, my parents were in attendance too, everyday, fashioning their destiny through hard work and dogged perseverance. My mother piloted the office desk and phone; my father sold and estimated jobs and toted and lugged furniture. In the final analysis, however, it was he, our drayman, who lent the stability, permanence, and real substance to their sustained labor, as our small family business grew up and came of age with the town itself.

He didn't at all resemble a rough-and-tumble furniture mover. Suited up in a starched collar and tie he could have easily passed as a shopowner, an optician, or even a pharmacist, save for his hands which would have given him away. Their calloused toughness telegraphed emphatically that he was a man who knew the meaning of hard, physical work.

Five and one-half feet he stood, not an inch more, and he fought throughout his working life to keep one hundred and thirty pounds stretched upon his wiry frame. Those summer days in the van could melt ten pounds a day off a granite tombstone, so one could imagine the difficulty a mortal encountered maintaining body weight in that sweltering environment. He was already graying and balding in his mid-thirties, when I first met him, a condition which had begun shortly after his twentieth birthday he confessed to me. He had china blue eyes and sported a freely pleasant smile which spread with happy and innocent contagion across his full, round face.

When my father's business could afford it, he was provided a uniform for work, as he quickly became our foreman, the only foreman — our Man Friday for all days of the week. The uniform rarely varied over the years. It was delivered by a laundry truck each week to the warehouse in a brown, wrapped bundle. This package contained a rigidly starched pair of gray pants and a short-sleeved, monogrammed, cotton work shirt. To this two-piece utility he added purple suspenders, a sleeveless, white undershirt, ghastly maroon rayon socks, and stiff brown workshoes.

He dressed out in that identical work attire for so long that I have no other mental recollection of his countenance.

The gray pants, ramrod straight, swam on his slender waist, supported precariously by the harness of suspenders which was forever coming loose through brushing encounters with furniture. His pants always looked as though they would plummet any moment all the way to his skinny shins but they never did. I always guessed the starch endured alone in keeping them properly up without the assistance of suspenders.

His flimsy socks, wet with perspiration, would invariably roll down and curl up at his ankles, revealing chalk-white stalks for legs, which simply couldn't, it appeared, uphold the lifting, shoving, lurching, dragging, pushing work demanded of their attached upper body. They did support him somehow, however, by some miraculous and unfathomed law of physics.

My buddies and I, throughout our high school summer vacations, and later, during summers at home in our college years worked on my father's trucks. I worked because I had to work. I had tried hiding, cowering as a puppy hearing running bath water, but living right on top of the business, I was always found and summoned. There was always, it seemed, a truck rumbling in to be loaded or unloaded.

My buddies worked because in those days, long before sophisticated Nautilus training and supervised weight-lifting conditioning programs came into vogue, staying in shape for school sports meant finding the toughest job you could find in the summer.

When we worked, there was never any doubt who was in charge. He was the foreman; we were the laborers. I demonstrated no inclination for driving the trucks and my father never pushed me in that direction, fearing perhaps that I would become a long-distance truck driver if I were allowed to drive them. Back-breaking labor on my part was sufficient enough for his approving eye and his molding design for me.

Every summer, from age fourteen well into my early twenties, I worked at the elbow of our foreman. Before age fourteen and his arrival, I had assisted, with small boy gaucherie, my father, with the hauling of bulky freight from railroad cars.

During those interminably long summer days, our truck would usually relocate each day two complete households of furniture. We seldom returned to the company warehouse anytime close to the appointed quitting time. The days extended well into the evenings and the grunting work, grimy and filthy, was pantingly arduous.

Often when we finally finished, we were too tired to go out at night on a date or to even enjoy a late supper. We slumped haggardly at our kitchen tables. Almost half of the local moving for the year took place in the summer months, between Memorial Day and Labor Day, permitting relocation to coincide with children out of school so that their educations could resume anew in September without undue interruption.

"Plenty of room! C'mon back! To the right a little! Got ten feet, whoa!" I would shout up to him from my position behind the truck, in helping to direct the backing of the grinding truck down driveways, or across lawns, dodging tree limbs, power lines, and overhanging branches. I never saw him hit anything he wasn't supposed to hit. He seemed to know just how far roof cornices and tentacled tree branches jutted out, judging expertly his safe distance through his rearview mirror, or with a regardant, gauging measurement, half slung out his driverside door.

The raucous clatter of the tailgate chain always disturbed me when it was dragged through metal eyelets to allow its lowering so that the work for the day could commence officially. The harsh, grating sound in early morning rudely broke a quiet neighborhood serenity. Its clank was the first, indelible reminder that a long day of groaning, sweating toil was stretching eternally before you.

We commoners, lowly helpers all, would unlock the refrigerator dolly from its metal coffin on the undercarriage of the truck, gather pliers and screwdrivers from the toolbox under the front seat in the cab, and putter with loose ropes and pads. He, usually accompanied by the lady of the house, would make a quick but thorough survey of the house in order to catalogue what possessions were to be entrusted to our temporary custody and what items, if any, were to be left alone.

He would scurry through the house, ma'aming this and ma'aming that, snorting with polite nervousness. He would rifle off courteous inquiries on what was to go and what was to stay, darting into room after room, down hallways, peeking into bulging closets, checking utility rooms for appliances, mentally assessing what pieces might jigsaw where in the cavern of truck. The canvas of the house was usually a one time occurrence. His trained eyes were everywhere, sizing and judging everything that we would handle.

We boys would gather in a knot outside, behind the truck, sequestered from his view. We would recite the morning sports news, rattling off batting averages and other sports minutiae, or we might lapse into some concocted war story about our latest female infatuation. Suddenly, jostled from our lulling daydream, we would hear him bound up the oaken walkboard calling for furniture, and we would hop to it, knowing there was no longer any way to delay the inevitable start of the workday.

After assuming his sacred role as chief packer and stacker,

he would return inside the house again only when we lesser mortals slowed up his flow of stackable goods for the hungry truck. Then, he would clomp down the plank again like a pirate leader, sniffing nervously. Motioning that we college numbskulls follow closely behind, he would go back into the house finding all manner of forgotten items for our open hands and idle, dangling arms. He would scold us playfully with quivering jowls and clicking teeth.

"Goodness gracious," he would whisper privately to each, out of earshot from the others, poking us in the ribs with a creased and leathered index finger while perspiration sprayed from his sopping forehead. "I've taught you everything I know, and you still don't know nothin'!"

We would bust up with rollicking laughter. This famous line, his trademark, we had heard a thousand times when we fouled up, but we never tired of having him say it in his own inimitable way.

If the day were sunny, we would bring the small and middling items out into view so as not to double move the larger pieces like chests and sofas, which were always carted directly to the truck. We would stack this array of smaller goods in a fantail semi-circle off the stern of the truck. From his high perch, directing the flow of goods like an orchestra conductor, he would point and signal to individual pieces. While constantly hitching his suspenders, he would make bookends with his notched hands, showing us below the exact size of a piece he needed to lodge into the correct hole he had constructed.

Under his call of baton we would move various pieces up into the truck to be packed away, wrapped in a protective pad where appropriate, until unmasked later when the great doors swung open a few miles or only short blocks away.

If the day were rainy, we would stack the goods within his sight as best we could, under a protective carport or in a garage, and then smugly disappear again from his view. He was wise to our ways, however. He knew rainy weather slowed our progress which meant that the welcomed sight of the warehouse would be later that evening, perhaps much later, as the work had to be completed regardless of the weather. So, in rainy or threatening weather, a staccato of gunnery sergeant orders streamed down to us in unending succession from his headquarters battery in the truck.

"Beds broken down?" he would demand.

"All down," we would confidently reply.

"Mirrors off?"

"Getting the last one now."

"Washer hooked on dolly?"

"Belted up and ready when you are!" we would shout back.

"Rugs rolled?"

On it went. His oral examination of our ineptitude was shot down to us as a stern English teacher would harangue a class while diagramming sentences at a blackboard. We, with our lick-and-promise answers, really fashioned ourselves slippery enough to withstand his relentless cross-examinations. How puerile it was to notion that.

When he had checklisted all our possible human frailties in the art of furniture moving, he would shuffle down and, wiping his brown, scuffed workshoes at any and every doorway, gesture for us hapless privates to troop in formation, to follow obsequiously through another personal investigation of every room in order to expose our ninety-five percent solution to the needed one hundred percent approach to the business at hand.

He would peer up at us with half a twinkle, carding perspiration from his brow and chin with a wiping cup of hand, whispering earnestly, "Lord knows. Now that you got everything out, bring the rest out."

We had heard this matchless line a thousand times but his way of saying it always produced laughter. Psychologically motivated for a time by our wise mentor, we would attack our jobs like voracious jackals until the next time when we needed prodding again. Parading an avalanche of goods into view, sometimes we would even get ahead of his stacking ritual. When this occurred, he would wag his head, muttering like a doting old woman. We were stoically expressionless, though bubbling with mirth inside our middles.

The atmosphere on the truck was one of unspoken, mutual respect. His authority, never wielded tyrannically, was unquestioned and unchallenged. He was the ruler absolute, with his "school of hard knocks" diploma, forged on the anvil of grunting toil. We college boys knew our station and place. On the job, final decisions on all matters were his to make and never did we tread on this privilege. Even though I was the owner's only son and could have thrown my weight around, I never did. My father would have scalped me had I tried. Our drayman sensed his aura of authority and dispatched it with the unshirking aplomb of an intrepid sea captain.

Ever aware of the weight of certain articles of furniture, often he would back away a stocky, college athlete from the task of lugging a laden chest out from a house and up into the truck. It was embarrassing. Two, young lions, together fully three times his weight were positioned on one end of some nine-foot buffet, and he alone took up the vigil at the other end. With arms locked, knees bent, legs shuffling with the groaning weight, without the slightest capitulation to imagined defeat, the end result was always accomplished. Not once in all those years did I ever see him fail to lift and move what he chose to lift and move.

Once our truck was packed and loaded, local trips in it were a welcomed respite for all of us. Each morning at the little office, when the jobs for the day were dispatched by my father and mother, we knew instantly if our load went only a few blocks, or, thankfully, across town, giving us a priceless half-hour or so of travel time in which to recover from the enslavement of loading the truck.

We would all pile into the narrow truck cab, smelly and bedraggled in our soaking work clothes, often four of us sardined across the front. The unlucky fourth person to board had to root around for a remnant of seat, and that poor soul was accosted for the duration of any trip by the ever-moving gearshift stick which swayed as a cobra rising from a basket.

Late each week with the magical approach of the weekend, we young bucks would banter with him as we rode, rapping about upcoming fun we had planned for our day and a half recess which finally arrived each Saturday at noon. Plans for outings at the beach, dating in town, or just plain collapsing sleep kept hope focused in our brains during those unforgettable and unforgiving summer workdays. He would shake his head behind the steering wheel and click his teeth as if to say that such idleness just couldn't bring any good.

We would ask him about his weekend plans, hopeful that this living dynamo of work had just a modicum of weekend frivolity in him, but we would turn silent when he related his drab weekends to us. A dual feeling of awe and uneasiness would harbor within us. He would tell that he had a roof to repair, or a siding of wall to erect, or a bathtub to install. He did home improvements for others on weekends and for himself, too, as he accumulated rental properties, investments wrought for his future with frugal dollars remaining from his Spartan, parsimonious style of living.

We loved him but his steadfast diligence to work enervated our minds and made us uncomfortable. So, when he condescended to just shopping for used cars some weekends, we were relieved when we learned of such pedestrian adventures. Why it was almost decadent we scoffed, not adding to his seventy-hour summer work week, by frittering time away shopping for used cars.

He would buy old cars, tinker and fix them, and then sell them at a nice profit from a vacant lot facing a main highway behind my father's warehouse. He bought at least two cars from me, one of which was a little short of oil, I'm afraid. I was such a scatterbrain in my college days that this particular vehicle couldn't compete successfully for dollars for regular oil treatments, with those dollars assigned instead to girls and good times.

His weekly paychecks from my father would back up in his wallet uncashed. Two, three, four checks even, suffocated for air in his bulgy rear pants pocket. My father would have to remind him to put them through the bank so his business books would balance. His wallet teemed with green lettuce and folded checks when one peeked at it, if one were eagle-eyed and swift. His cobwebbed vault of leather didn't creak open very often.

During our crosstown trips, loaded and running for our destination, when lunch time brightened our daily bondage, we would all chorus an entreaty for him to stop at a grocery store so we could buy a quart of milk or a cool soda with which to wash down our bagged sandwiches which we had stowed under the seat in the cab that morning. He would protest mildly, saying we had to make time, but he would always stop. We would unpile and stumble inside some sparse market seeking liquid refreshment, our ears burning to his refrain, "Lord have mercy, hurry now, we're burning up daylight."

Once we conspired not to inveigle him into stopping at a store, to see if he would stop on his own. He was true to form; nothing asked for, nothing expected, and Millet's bent "The Man with a Hoe" was personified. He pulled the truck over on the shoulder of a dusty road after passing several grocery stores and we proceeded to have our lunch, dry and pasty. We learned our lesson and thereafter always asked him to stop. He wasn't punishing us, it just never occurred to him to stop to spend money for a drink.

There we sat that noon, forlorn in the sizzling Florida sun, munching our mealy, hastily constructed sandwiches, trying to lumpily hammer them down with saliva. He patiently unfolded his skimpy lunch from its crackling, creased brown bag, and after folding the bag again for future usage, he stolidly sat, silently devouring the paltry offering inside with relishing satisfaction.

It was during these hurried, truck-idling pauses at grocery stores that the stage occasionally set itself for his masterpiece in stalwart self-denial. He suffered from severe headaches and at these times, when he stopped to accommodate us, he would ask me to fetch him a headache powder. When I returned to the truck with it, he would roar off, gearing up from neutral on his relentless way, and deftly, with one hand free from the steering wheel, unpackage the cellophaned slug of dust. Calmly tilting back his head, keeping slitted eyes on the road, he would allow the entire potion to slide down the funneled wrapper into his mouth. We were speechless, eager for any grimace, primed for any clay-footed frown of humanness, but our pleas for salving oneness with ourselves were unrequited. With arched eyebrows and wrinkled noses we huddled in the cab reverently, silently returning the gaze of each other with wonder and disbelief whenever this self-mutilating and self-doctoring ritual took place.

Lunch time was spent differently when it didn't coincide with travel time. At those times, still loading, we took our lunch break in the partially filled, parked truck. We were allotted one-half hour for lunch, never more, and he kept track of those escaping company minutes with ardent awareness.

Sometimes I would persuade cool drinks from the lady of the house, usually ice water but now and then I would bound up the plank with a treasure trove of iced tea in a pitcher or a handful of cap-sprung sodas. Naturally, he never asked for a cool drink. His drinks came from the hot nozzles of green, coiled hoses, lounging like sleeping snakes on yards, or from bathroom sinks, where hinged at the waist, he slurped down tepid refreshment from cupped hands.

We helpers would rush madly through our lunch, ripping away wrappers, wolfing larger than bite-sized chunks of sandwiches as an early completion of lunch meant sleep, blessed sleep, during those humid, lazy summer lunch breaks. He would wag his head and tut-tut a teasing, pedagogic "boys will be boys" lament as we scurried about getting comfortable, sprawling anywhere we could find shade.

With furniture pad balled up as gamy pillow we would sink quickly into deep sleep without benefit of Brahms. He would munch away on his dry sandwiches, chewing incessantly with his strong cheek muscles inflated to maximum chipmunking expansion.

All would be quiet for a few minutes. We would drift off to the distant whirr of a neighborhood lawn mower or to the buzzing drone of a fat, blue fly. It was brief, that blessed sleeping respite, in the middle of those long workdays. All too soon, we would hear him stir about. No, it can't be, we would plead to ourselves with eyes tightly shut to reality. It just can't be.

He would rustle quietly at first, folding a rumpled pad, coiling a tie rope — silent things, as he loved us, and in his way, he was allowing us to gather a few more minutes of repose, protecting us like a scrubwoman who would rather labor long hours herself than have her child work through college.

But then, he would graduate to louder activities as lunch sleep had to conclude. Still we dozed and he let us doze, but now he made no effort to remain quiet. His little broom was flashing away on the slanted walkboard now; his cheap shoes were scuffing; he was humming and singing as he busied himself again. And then, suddenly, all at once, our Valhallan bastion of sleep was shattered with his bark.

"It's hard but it's fair!", he would adjudicate. "You had a good home but you wouldn't stay there." Poking us gently in the ribs with his broom or drawing a slender stalk of ragweed beneath our twitching noses, he would continue.

"This life and one more and then the hell really starts."

Complaining and whining, we would stand and stretch our limbs, which, to any nocturnal observer could have been seen jangling around the faithful, local watering hole the night before until the rooster side of midnight. Tethered by a plain, rawhide cord from a beltloop, he would retrieve his ancient timepiece from his starched watchpocket and announce the half-hour concluded to the dot, lest any slippage of sleep be debited to company time.

In the late 1950's, during the "cold war" with the Soviet Union, in the post-Korean War days when both countries were flexing their readied might frighteningly, the United States Air Force billeted many servicemen directly "on base," close to their airplanes. The feeling prevailed that close proximity to airplanes was essential for rapid retaliatory measures to succeed in the event of a surprise nuclear attack. My father's business was awarded part of this service contract, known as Capehart Housing in honor of Senator Homer Capehart of Indiana, and we were given a great deal of work at the airbases in our local area. How we worked, honoring our portion of that contract award! Those summer work days averaged twelve to fourteen hours in duration.

Many a night I stumbled to bed too weary to shower or even to eat. He, however, drayman ever unflappable and undaunted, would go about his job with the same sense of dutiful completion which characterized his performance during the more sane times of the year. Often, with the moon fully up, we college boys, sporting our third rank T-shirt of the day, bone tired, with sunken, circled eyes, would slump wearily into the stuffy cab of the truck or drape ourselves loosely over a cooling truck fender, spent with the realization that our date on the town that night would be impossible to keep. At those glum times, the only real solace we clung to in the welter of our cindered brains was that the work day was mercifully over, with only the twenty-mile drive back to the warehouse remaining before we could win our release for good behavior.

But was it over? Were we safe? He always made one, final

inspection through the house after every last stick of furniture had been set in place, regardless of the late hour. Usually the customers themselves were too tired from simply watching him work to have the audacity to ask him to do more. After wiping his feet at every doorway, he would sniff nervously through his memorized checklist, gesticulating with his raspy, rough-notched hands.

"Anythin' else we can do, ma'am?"

"No!"

"Want anythin' more unpacked?"

"No, thank you."

"Need anythin' rearranged?"

"No, really. Everything's fine."

"All your rugs in place and mirrors back on dressers?"

"Yes, really, it's fine. You boys run along now, it's late," was the customary and welcomed reply. Occasionally, though, when something needed doing at those late hours, something that undoubtedly could have been avoided, were it not for his punctilious adherence to duty, he would call us back into the house, awakening us from our zombied stupor. We would stumble in, trooping along like beaten, unkempt soldiers.

Usually though, late at night, he alone did what needed to be done, realizing our tired condition made us susceptible to sloppy work and irritability in front of the customers. When the last iota of vexing chore was completed, he would lope back to the truck, swing up into his seat clutching an assortment of screwdrivers, pliers, and wrenches we had left scattered throughout the house and scold us playfully with the same energy he had possessed at break of day that morning.

Handyman extraordinaire was he. The onslaught of summer, with people madly relocating their addresses while children were out of school, did not last all year. His rare, divergent talents surfaced during those somewhat less frantic months of the year. He tinkered with engines, half hidden from view in the bowels of a truck. He painted and fumigated warehouses, routed septic tank lines at the end of a shovel, dug up tree stumps, mowed grass, swept floors, repaired machinery, assembled wooden crates, shingled roofs, added rooms on our house, and even babysat.

When trucks were abandoned around the county by the irresponsibility of imbibing long-distance truck drivers, my father would suit him up smartly, and with suitcase in hand, my mother would drive him to the airport so he could fetch home the stranded truck from its reported inertness in another state.

Seldom did he ask for a thing. Many times I felt sorry for him, breaking in new helpers year after year, never really working with anyone who approximated his leonine heart for work, having always to explain and instruct, often doing the job of another as well as his own.

When early September arrived each year, I would gladly return to college, packing my stylish Chevrolet coupe with crewneck sweaters, white buck shoes, buckled-in-the-back slacks and all my bat and glove paraphernalia for varsity baseball. Thankful was I to trade those glorious, nor-so-dismal textbooks for that endless parade of summer furniture.

He would wish me well, implore me to study hard, and speed me on my way with a heartfelt farewell. He was always genuinely interested in my welfare. His eyes would twinkle mischievously when he quizzed me about the college girls, interrogating me jokingly about any nocturnal conquests the previous year. I would back out from our driveway near the warehouse, honk goodbye, and receive a long parting wave from him as he craned his round, smiling face out and around the corner of an open truck door.

For two decades he orchestrated my father's business. When my father sold his business, he spent a dozen years with another moving and storage company, which conducted business nearby in the larger city adjacent to our little town. He established his indomitable indispensability with the new employer in a short matter of time.

Over the years I would drop in on him occasionally to keep tabs on his life and to glean from him the local scuttlebutt. At his little cottage, we would spin yarns of the past with our elbows braced on the sideboard of his red pickup and shoots of grass lolling in our mouths. Our most rollicking laughter highlighted the rememberance of the afternoon he found me on the job in a darkened bedroom, which had been relieved of its furniture with only me left behind, lying on the floor with my feet propped up against the wall, enjoying a lengthy conversation with my girlfriend on the solitary phone which had not been disconnected in the barren room.

Then there was the infamous Mrs. Potter incident, the day I thought my life would end at the advanced age of nineteen. My father was upstairs in Mrs. Potter's ancient frame house, estimating the cost of the moving job for the dear, sweet lady. My buddy and I had started transporting pieces down the narrow, rickety staircase. We could hear my father's voice oiling Mrs. Potter with assurances that the job would be performed expertly. Just then the clumsy, overstuffed sofa we were lugging downstairs lodged firmly in the stairwell. We couldn't budge it. Billowing dust from the bruised walls clouded the air as we struggled. The staircase handrail sprung a screw as we jostled the long sofa in an attempt to free it. My buddy on the top end started laughing, purpling uncontrollably. His convulsion wildfired to me below him and I caved to a heap of hysterical, muted laughter at the bottom of the stairs, framing couplets for my tombstone epitaph with my father surely about to practice filicide once he discovered our clumsy predicament.

In the early 1980's, our drayman mulled the thought of retirement. At age sixty-five he had begun to feel in his bones the crunching ordeal of daily labor on the trucks. His new company pleaded for just one more year of service; and, of course he relented and obliged them. Amid that whirlpool of retirement talk, desired earnestly by him each year, and cajolingly tabled by the company gavel each year in rebuttal, I gave him a fusillade of all my accumulated wisdom. I was in rare form, angry and forceful with my pulpitized soliliquy.

"You have earned retirement," I preached. "Remember last summer? They talked you into staying only one more year, and you gave in to them. Don't waver again. They'll whine and say they can't get along without you, but they can! Be firm and call it quits."

He sniffed, squinched his blue eyes, serrated a blade of grass with his teeth, and pawed silently at a clod of earth with the blunt toe of a cheap, brown shoe.

"Let me tell you about companies," I warned, hammering a fist on his red pickup. "They pay us sure, allowing us to buy things, but remember, companies endure but people like ourselves, who build them, die early. Companies are brick, block, and stone. We are only glue, mortar, and pitch. We disintegrate in time. They remain, perhaps cracked and scarred, but they remain. We, who hold them together, are replaced.

We do not long survive. This year, be polite but be firm — tell them 'no' this time."

I paused, winded, and looked at him deeply through his eyes. Slowly, he stuttered assurances to me that he would definitely quit, averting shyly my eyes as he spoke. I put my hand down on his scanty shoulder and sighed. I had been speaking to a gatepost.

Finally, two years after my speech, he did retire. Someone close to him arranged for a feature story of his life in the local newspaper. His picture for the article, taken alongside his trusty, blunt-nosed Chevrolet truck, was a modern "American Gothic" without the pitchfork. Thank God his suspenders were neat across his shoulders for the picture.

There was no clamor, no tribute, no gold watch when he retired, all of which he richly deserved. The hundreds of people who called over the years and asked my mother in the dispatch office to "send the little old man," or "is that wonderful foreman still with you, you know the one, send him," never knew of his retirement.

No mythical dinner at some swank hotel was ever held. No Samuel Gompers, John L. Lewis, or Walter Reuther were in attendance on a festooned dais honoring him in a manner that would have been fitting, given his unswerving contribution to the plodding, honest march of devoted unknowns through the smithy of American labor.

When I learned of his retirement, I rushed out to see him and we, once again, set up our whimsical bar-without-drinks on the fender of his red pickup. We tabulated together perhaps a total of 12,000 moving jobs with him in command as foreman. We listed astoundingly, an estimation of 500 helpers with whom he labored, many of them totally useless, having to be dragged along at their jobs.

He told me of a little plot of land in Tennessee, with a house trailer sitting in the shade — a hideaway which he planned to farm in the summers.

I beat my drum of persuasion again.

"Great," I said. "Stay active. Don't let us hear about some new retiree kicking the bucket, bored in his retirement with nothing to do." Then red-faced, I caught myself, realizing the utter lunacy of my warning.

"Listen to me, will you? I'm sorry. Stay busy? You? You'll always stay busy."

* * *

The college boys who worked with us went on to own businesses, coach college athletics, run banks, conduct scientific experiments, write books, approach robed judges at the bar, and even dangle stethoscopes around their necks, but in all my life, I never met a better man than our local drayman.

He wasn't perfect. Thank God for that. I wouldn't lock that suffocating, stumbling yoke on the shoulders of anyone. To me, however, he was a heroic triumvirate of Captain Marvel, Superman, and Batman — a model which has endured all my life. He zoomed through the sky of my youth, his tired suspenders and bony shoulders sprouting a majestic cape, community movingman extraordinaire, our unforgettable drayman, kind and wise king over all his vassals and all the worldly possessions entrusted to his special care.

He was simple clay that became a museum vase.

THE LIGHT FROM THE MEZZANINE

The gleaming, tourist-jammed, excursion bus crawled to a hissing stop along the curving margin of black asphalt at the main entrance to the fancy, downtown hotel. Its wide door levered open with a metallic gasp unleasing a bath of cold, manufactured air to fend alone for its survival, outside in scorching Florida June.

One would have thought an important international celebrity were aboard, so condescendingly gracious were most of the hotel greeters, middle-management flunkies clamoring to welcome the arriving bus. There were arm-pumping hellos at the base of the steps, offers to an unsure elbow here, fingers pointing directions there. Sky-venturing balloons escaped from small hands in the hot breeze, as tiny heads tilted back to try to see the top of the grand hotel.

There were no celebrities aboard, no sheiks, no foreign ministers, no stateside dignitaries of any description — only sixty-five, wide-eyed Americans from a sparkplug factory town in Ohio who had hoarded pennies and nickels, squirreled away for two years in cupboard mason jars, so they could enjoy eight enchanting days, sightseeing in Central Florida.

Only Tom Phillips, among the press corps of hotel people, seemed genuinely interested in the bedraggled throng, now pretzeling out stiffly from their confinement on the highway. Tom, tallish and slim, dressed modestly in a stylish dark suit, was cheerful and friendly in fielding the questions chattered in his direction.

He wasn't as gooey with his answers as were his middle-management cohorts, who were peacocking their replies with doctored insincerity, largely for the benefit of the tinted mezzanine windows directly above them. It was whispered that top management executives often lurked behind those windows, standing opaquely there, assessing the forced ardor of the hotel staff below, when the great buses puffed in to belch forth new loads of worn travelers with itchy money in their pockets.

The pressure to please the arriving guests, perks relentlessly dredged up by managerial persuasions, was most intense each year between Memorial Day and Labor Day, and then again from Thanksgiving through New Year's Day. These were the "crunch times" as they were labeled by airports, travel bureaus, and the harried staffs who held together the gaudy hotels in Central Florida.

Eager, competent, and quietly efficient at the hotel, Tom performed his duties with a minimum of wasted movement. His counterparts, two scrubbed, young men nearly his own age, and two equally correct sparkling corporate women, always seemed to work harder than Tom in placating the tour managers and with the routine matters of supplying directions to the nearest drugstore, or liquor store, or worse, having to apologize dumbly for not knowing some Aunt Gertrude in the local area when cornered by well-meaning tourists in that horrible "do-you-know-our-relatives" scenario.

The heat was on everyone, definitely outside in the swelter of late June, but inside, too, as that month the watchword had gone out, coined by some fiendish executive, "Live '87, Be '87."

The downtown hotel was madly finishing a satellite hotel,

closer to the world-famous theme park. It was to be completed in 1987 for the summer tourist banquet that year. Either Tom or one of the other four, eager lieutenants, busy among the touristing troops, would be selected this coming Labor Day for the number two slot at the new edifice, a stepping-stone coup that decreed with certainty that the lofty, celestial heights of top management were inevitable for the future if one were only to do a fair job and, most importantly, keep their nose sponged reasonably clean.

Tom guessed that he was in the hunt for the position, a position being called magical and utterly crucial by everyone, who knew anything about it. Eight years out of college, winner there of the business fraternity plaque his senior year in the field of *HOTEL MANAGEMENT,* and well-entrenched now, at only his second career stop, Tom, banging on the bittersweet door of his thirtieth birthday, assumed shruggingly that he was as logical a choice as any.

Into early July, when passing Tom along the deep, silent carpeting, top management treated him to an urging smile and raised fist in reciting aloud their pet slogan, "Live '87, Be '87." Tom would smile back at them, remain mostly silent, and continue expertly with his duties. Often top management would stop and pivot to peer inquiringly after Tom, and with suited arms akimbo on their ample hips, they wondered why Tom hadn't balled a fist like the others, championing back, "Live '87, Be '87." Tom wasn't one to snuggle up to management, they pouted, but they all freely admitted among themselves that his work was outstanding.

The summer buzzed along. The great buses, silver ships of the land, snorted in constantly, disgorging their fretting menagerie of human anticipation — those chalky white of arm and leg, pillowed pudgy at the tummy, and crowned with every contraption of gaudy chapeau imaginable. A few days later, the same mass of visitation stumbled back to board identical buses, whiningly pink or red of arm and leg, further puffed at their jiggling tummies, and bedecked with a different, local assortment of horrid, cheap hats.

Amid the clamor that reigned in the lobby of the hotel, crying children dislodging stacked luggage, jibbering parents trying to fold road maps as large as kitchen tables, one morning in early July, an exhibit of twelve paintings arrived. They were delivered by a moving van, uncrated knee-deep in padded excelsior, and threaded through the thronging lobby carefully, one at a time, by two white-gloved moving men who stepped reverantly. The paintings were attached along the mezzanine wall by the caressing, soft hands of local art society members, who emerged incongruously through the milling lobby in long pants and skirts to orchestrate the procedure.

It took nearly a day for all twelve paintings to be positioned correctly along the mezzanine wall, outside the executive suites and among the several conference room doors which faced out upon that balconied floor. The art enthusiasts, deaf to the raucous din of restless tourists half a floor below, took their time with the hanging arrangements.

When they finished and were satisfied, each painting, equidistant from another and at the correct viewing height, displayed itself proudly in its assigned place. A neat, unobtrusive placard, tilted on a gold stand near the top of the mezzanine staircase, explaining the exhibit for those who would steal a glance from a busy moment to read it, completed their fussy love affair.

Tom read the placard the first day it was displayed and had

every intention to admire the twelve paintings. He knew he would do so, given a free, waking moment from his demanding routine, but then, as always, it seemed, he was conveyed along by the endless crunch of new visitors. The queue of silver buses lengthened throughout late July and into early August. During the humid drone of summer, Tom found himself catching quick cups of coffee in the snack shop, alone and perplexed. Before the prize of second-in-command at the satellite hotel had been announced, as the priceless brass ring of top management, the five young executives on the "go-go" squad had been bound as one, spirited together with daily camaraderie at their jobs.

Now, however, during the last, broiling weeks of summer, with the managerial selection slated for the Tuesday after Labor Day, Tom was startled to find himself snubbed by the other four aspirants for the position. He wasn't ostracized, just apart, as all the others chose to be apart from any of the other four. Tom was glad, at least, that the snubbing seemed to show no favoritism — it was uniformly distant for all.

Whenever he was the first to arrive in the snack shop, he would signal his location to any of the other four when they arrived. Often, certain he had been seen, he was astonished to see them plop on a counter stool by themselves, or scoot into a vacant booth across the room. When he was late arriving, no hailing wave came from any of them.

The hammering, managerial blare of "Live '87, Be '87" had splintered their union, shattering their mutual bond into flimsy kindling wood. Tom became saddened as the days of torrid summer limped along, unhappy with the competitive yoke forced upon the group by the catchy slogan. The five became mentally separated, onerously and imperceptibly driven to corners, as wise captors segregate officers from enlisted men in wartime.

As the summer progressed with its days of endless sunlight, Tom continued his duties with mercurial efficiency, performing them smoothly in his inimitable style of little wasted motion. Somehow he was able to largely blot out the mysterious change in the other four, their coolness for each other.

The top executives no longer pouted when they occasioned Tom in an elevator or on a staircase when he failed to salute with a balled fist and a lusty "Live '87, Be '87." They shook their heads lamely, sighing with some economic comfort in the fact that whirlwind Tom turned out excellent work even if he didn't cuddle up to top management. They smiled after him as he hurdled new pots of steaming coffee on stainless steel carts through the accordioned conference room doorways and when he balanced trays of swirly pastries through rooms teeming with bleary-eyed conventioneers.

At his condominium on Friday nights, Tom regressed to charcoaling steaks alone, poking at them moodily for his date and himself. Formerly, on Friday nights, before the announcement of the satellite hotel position, the team of five and their various dates had chipped together, devouring truckloads of delivered pizzas when slumming, or dicing up some culinary masterpiece together, step by step from a dog-eared page in someone's cookbook, when they felt especially ritzy.

Things were definitely not the same. That blasted satellite hotel, that sweet-whispering Siren of promise, had drawn them apart, quartering them distantly as a stern proctor in some huge, examination auditorium separates students in order to monitor cheating.

Tom resigned himself to his new ostracism those last wilting weeks of August, although he did not come to find it agreeable with his nature. The last few days toasted along slowly to that momentous Tuesday after Labor Day. He took his coffee alone in the snack shop, propped intently behind copies of *Hotel and Motel News*. He found it best to have his eyes busy so the others wouldn't redden in trying to avoid his greetings. However, throughout the chameleon of change with the others, when eyes met inevitably, Tom was always the first with a wave and a smile as though no bridges had been burned.

The *Hotel and Motel News* helped Tom cope with his melancholic state. He didn't brood but laughed instead when he browsed the classified ads about running some mom-and-pop motel at the beach or in the mountains for aging, arthritic owners, advertising for new, vibrant energy at the helm. What a world apart were some of these quaint situations, from the beehiving terminal of tourism which ruled his consciousness now.

Finally, after nearly four months of agonizing wail and much dishrag-wrung anxiety supplied tensely by the other four hopefuls and top management, the first Tuesday after Labor Day claimed its square on the calendar. The screaming kids were back in school, dragged back there by sun-blistered parents, who were irritable now with itchy clothes and the escaping subtraction in their vacation checkbooks. The tourist faucet was off with unleaking alacrity.

The hotel restocked stolen towels, bed linen, and an occasional filched lamp and repaired their glittering facades for the next tidal wave of guests which would come flooding in when the great, stuffed bird would grace Thanksgiving tables.

Tom was assigned final interview slot number four. Three hopefuls were ahead of him, and one aspirant for the coveted position would endure the vigil behind him. All were told that the interviews would being at 4:00 p.m. and follow one another sequentially, every twenty minutes. Tom calculated his time for summons behind the foreboding doors on the mezzanine as approximately 5:00 p.m.

He arrived on the mezzanine at 4:35 p.m., finding it largely deserted at that quiet off-hour. The very last trickle of summer hoard was away, still wringing the theme parks for that last droplet of fun. He shared the rose-pink corridor with Miss Warren, interviewee number three before him, a former close confidante with whom he had shared many a laugh, but who, alas, had fallen now on zombie times these last few months, coming to wear a drawn white shade for a face where brooks of merriment had bubbled before.

Tom hailed her with a greeting. Stiffly seated on a padded bench, fidgety and pale, she managed a weak smile, a brief upward curve to her blank countenance. A cold statue, she was gnawing her nails with a voracity that would achieve Venus de Milo status for her arms in only a matter of minutes. He made no further conversational overture, allowing her, especially now, the solitary space she had seemed to seek the last few weeks.

With his hands clasped behind him, Tom drifted away silently, sauntering along the mezzanine balcony. He decided to study the paintings he had been meaning to enjoy. A close inspection of the scrolled placard encouraged him, as the display was scheduled for removal from the mezzanine in only a matter of days. Parading back and forth all summer on his daily rounds, he had given the paintings a polite "once-over" since their arrival, certainly showing more interest than any other hotel official had seen fit to display, but now he had time to accord them the true "museum-on-a-rainy-afternoon" treatment.

They were natural settings, breathtaking and majestic, detailed gloriously with exacting brushwork. Each was trimmed neatly by a plain, wooden frame surrounding a white, mat border. There was something hauntingly distinctive about them, but Tom couldn't quite pinpoint what it was. Each was signed by the same artist, precisely, in the lower right corner, just above a mention of date.

There was a disturbing wonder about them. Tom sorted with it, mused over it, and finally, unresolved with it, catalogued its mystery within his subconscious mind, hopeful the answer would pop out for him.

Down the corridor the double doors of the "Live '87, Be '87" Inquistion opened. Tom glanced toward them. His previous, close friend, Phil Baxter, appeared at the opening, head held aloft in obvious defeat. He strode wordlessly down the plush carpeting, as a nobleman snooty to the end despite an unswerving appointment with the guillotine. Obviously he had been rejected for the prized position by the august body of hotel hierarchy.

Rallied by Phil's apparent misfortune, Kimberly Warren, candidate number three, rose quickly, brushed her suit, where she had sat, adjusted her immaculate coiffure with fluffing fingers, and pranced as a colt at first dawn, awaiting the call to enter through the double doors.

"Miss Warren," summoned a bodyless voice somewhere inside the doorway. She marched forward into her future.

Tom returned to his study of the paintings. The perplexing mystery about them tumbled in his skull. They were beautiful, but there was just something about them. What was it? Tom cocked his head to the left, then to the right. He viewed them from different angles, walking close up, and then retreating back to the balcony railing to ponder that perspective. At the end of the corridor, arriving as candidate number five, Tony Alvarez sagged into the still warm, padded bench vacated by Miss Warren. Tony would be last, after Tom. Long-suffering with his greetings, Tom politely hailed Tony as he had Kimberly Warren, but Tony did not look his way. Rather, he busied himself sorting his wallet credit cards on his lap, passing the time checking for expiration dates among his stack of plastic booty. Tom pursed his lips and sighed wearily. Kimberly and Tony were practically strangers now. Such fun he had shared with the two of them on a Labor Day canoe trip almost exactly a year ago.

Saddened again with the change in both Kimberly and Tony, Tom forced his attention back to the paintings. The signature on each one was bold and sharp. There was a date on each, below the artist's signature, consisting of a numeral, apparently for the month, then a diagonal slash and another numeral, undoubtedly noting the actual day that the easel had been tripoded before the scene to be captured on canvas.

"Hmm," mouthed Tom. "September 23rd on this one, number 9, slash, number 23. Yes, I see it — just a hint of autumn, no real color change with the leaves. Summer's last gasp."

Tom paced off eight feet to one side and halted at the next painting. He peered in at the signature and the date below it. The date read number 6, slash number 11. Tom backed away half the distance to the railing to drink in the scene.

"Yes, early summer up north. Not the blister of July or August — the sun not ablaze, just warm. Early summer. That fisherman still in a light sweater." Tom announced to himself that he probably could have guessed that month without the date assistance on the painting.

Tom measured eight more feet down the corridor, eager to analyze the third painting.

"Winter, unmistakably, but," added Tom, hesitantly, groping about to unlock, unknowingly, an elusive and enthralling puzzle in his mind, "which month of winter — early winter, deep winter, or winter before the thaw?"

Tom placed a hand over his mouth pensively and wrinkled his brow.

"I'll try December, before Christmas — light snow, but not deep in rock crevices where it could have built up for months. Brook not frozen. Some sparse patches of vegetation. I'll spring for December 12, just for fun."

He edged forward, eager to detect the actual date. He was warming to his new game as he awaited those final minutes before his audience in the conference room. The painting was vintage 12/8. Tom broke into a broad smile and hurried eight feet further, to the fourth painting.

"Spring ... but Spring is ninety days long." He gave himself little hope of beating his four-day closeness to the December date on the previous painting, but he was spurred to try. He studied this one intently, from every angle, as a golfer would study a championship putt on the final green. He bent down, hinged his waist, bobbed his head, and narrowed his eyes. Childlike, he was almost gleeful, forgetting the weighty gravity of the moment, in possibly being the choice for "Live '87, Be '87."

Tony didn't notice Tom's antics. He had dropped all of his credit cards on the carpet and was collecting them again, cursing to himself.

Tom submitted his scorecard for the fourth painting. "I'll say March 22nd. Buds back on ... a real skinny bear ... some float ice ... snow only in patches. The date was scribed 3/28. Six days off. Who's really good here, the artist or me?" Tom laughed.

Now absorbed with the intriguing guesswork of the times of the year depicted by the artist, Tom was tantalized by the eight remaining paintings. He had read two dates, days in some September and June, but he had legitimately guessed two others, days in someone's December and March.

Still, something perplexed Tom. He couldn't quite isolate what it was. It was as though he were hearing a melodious tune in his brain, a hauntingly pleasant bit of music from his youth, familiar but distant, unnamed as a definite recollection.

"Now here's a rough one," scoffed Tom. If the others wouldn't talk with him, he would talk with himself, he decreed.

"It has to be the middle of the summer, but when?" Tom had begun to realize that the paintings dated near the shift of seasonal change were easier to pinpoint because of the telltale signs provided. This one was tough.

"The cauldron of summer. Sawgrass at the seashore drooping to the sand like necks of horses in a parched pasture. Car packed for home. Children on vacation. But, is it Memorial Day weekend, Fourth of July, or Labor Day weekend ... or worse for someone trying to guess, just some obscure day cooking along in hot summer that would be even more difficult to determine?"

Tom was stumped. He was just about to circle July fourth on the testpage in his mind.

"No, wait! Wooden shutters stacked under windows ready

to go back up . . . claw hammer out — traditional end of summer at the shore up north. Sure, The shore it's called up there; the beach down here. It shuts up again up there at Labor Day." Tom snapped his fingers, delighted with his detective work.

Tony glanced up at the sound from down the corridor and grimaced at Tom's exuberance, thinking Tom had some flashing revelation for his own upcoming interview that could wrest glory away from himself.

"Eureka!" exclaimed Tom, slapping his right thigh. "It has to be Labor Day. I'll say September second."

Tom stepped forward confidently and recited the date aloud.

"September third — off by one day. I should be the curator at the Louvre."

Tom bore on, hastening down the balcony, putting more distance between himself and squirming Tony.

"Ugh, another tough one, camouflaged deep in the ninety day season of winter. How can I do this one?" he shrugged with surrendering hands limp at his sides.

"Naked, gaunt trees . . . round mounds of snow . . . icicles like white carrots . . . dead of winter. Could be wrong by a month. February, I guess." He groaned.

"Wait. By the driveway of these two brick cottages near the mailboxes, two browning, conical trees are tipped on their sides. Of course, Christmas trees out for the trash people after the holidays. Not February — January! Let's pick, say, . . . January eighth."

Tom marched forward apprehensively, as a raw recruit in a military induction line, awaiting hypodermic needles pointed for each, bare arm.

January sixth was the date. Two days off. Tom kicked back his head and chuckled lightly, and bathed his face in a curling smile.

Tony writhed on his padded bench down the corridor, shifting and squirming with as much placidity as a sunburned, potbellied tourist with an active case of hemorrhoids.

Tom scooted laterally to the next painting. His summons for his interview was, at most, five minutes away.

"Oh, God," he stammered. "Oh, God, it's right there and I didn't see it."

A damp film of mental purgation broke through his epidermis into the honest light of day. It glistened across his forehead, moistened his hands, flushed his face, and riveleted with prickled sensor right down to his wiggling toes.

"Oh, God," he repeated. He couldn't stop saying, "Oh, God."

He placed the slick palm of one hand over his eyes and slowly drew it down over his face. Its descending passage flattened his nose and distorted his lips, before it ended in a final, clutching grasp at his collared throat.

"OH, GOD — THERE ARE NO YEARS! NO YEARS! So obvious, yet I wouldn't see — just months and days, the moments of our lives. No cold, labeled silos embossed with the numeral of some lousy year where the rich wheat of moments is forgotten in storage. No "Live '87, Be '87." No years of any description.

Tom knifed a hand into the air, and congratulated himself.

"It is the journey in life, yes the journey itself, not the goal set for you, usually by someone else. The journey, yes, the marvelous journey."

"Of course, I didn't see at first. It is the days of March, or June, or November which are sacred in their proud individuality, not the unfeeling years which try to categorize them. No 1066, 1588, 1812, 1861, 1914, 1941, 1945 — years we were forced to remember in school, dates of the Norman Conquest, the Spanish Armada, the War of 1812, the outbreak of our Civil War, World War I beginning, Pearl Harbor, or the year of the mushrooming atomic cloud. No cold dates to highlight war and agony — NO YEARS!"

Tom didn't miss a month. He correctly picked an October scene within three days of the artist's date mark. He was fully three weeks off on a July painting, and eighteen days away from the artist's conception of a November afternoon, but he had seen and seen well, understanding and deeply appreciating the intent of the artist.

The collection was a masterpiece in subtlety, a free expression of artistic talent depicting days and months of our lives — moments, moments, moments. Tom further realized that the paintings were randomly hung, not successively January through December down the corridor. That must have been the brilliant design of the art society, not to form any regimental year with them, as they had taken such time and care in positioning them the day they arrived.

"I see," panted Tom. "All twelve, neatly but randomly hung, expressing the artist's desire for joyous moments unto themselves, free from the encapsulating rigidity of all twelve linked and fettered by suggestion into any one constraining year. Marvelous!"

The doors of the conference room opened quietly, almost reverantly, discharging an unpromoted, teary-faced Miss Kimberly Warren back out once again to the balconied corridor. She twisted away from Tom and Tony, weaving toward the staircase, blinded by the salty liquid which was obscuring her vision and smudging her makeup.

"I guess it's Tony or me," breathed Tom ventriloquially, now loathing their pet slogan, "Live '87, Be '87."

Tony, wriggling on his bench, tallied the same conclusion with Miss Warrens' rapid departure. He shot sidelong daggers of vanity through Tom's heart. Then he fidgeted roughly with his tie, further darkening his swarthy face as he cinched it tighter against his collar. He shook his wrists so that exactly one-half inch of exposed shirt sleeve peeked out below the arms of his dark suit.

"Mr. Phillips," proctored the voice at the double doors. Tom was led into the room. Six, seated men formed a horseshoe around an oval, mahogany table upon which an iced pitcher of water, surrounded by a dozen inverted glasses, perspired as centerpiece on a silver tray.

The room, richly tapestried by wall, and deeply cushioned by floor, was bereft of extra furniture. Its one, large eye of window was lidded with a folded droop of heavy drapery. Tom was offered the one vacant chair at the open base of their horseshoe. He sat.

"Tom, I'll come right to the point," pompously began the graying executive, standing lordly now as spokesman at the top of the horseshoe assemblage.

"Are you prepared to 'Live '87, Be '87,' meaning, are you prepared to work harder than you've ever thought of working in your life?" He emphatically knifed one pink and manicured hand into the tender palm of his other.

Tom remained silent, expressionless — practically catatonic, unable to reply. The pause was somewhat awkward. The spokesman managed a weak laugh. The other five responded in kind, with forced and reserved splatters of polite coughing, and they shifted their ample bottoms to new positions on their conference room chairs.

"Now, Tom" he pursued, "one thing that we all have always liked about you, well, that is, to put it bluntly, well, you never really court top management like the others." He waved casually in the direction of the mezzanine balcony.

Still Tom said nothing. The clean, introspective bath of those twelve paintings was drenching him as a waterfall shower, tumbling and gurgling down over rocks in some dense jungle haven after a vine-slapping tramp of many miles.

The six men claimed Tom intently, clasping him with a curious, collective stare. As if on cue from offstage prompter, they leaned forward ever so slightly in their chairs.

"Thank you," Tom said, painfully attentive to the business at hand. He had to say something.

The group smiled smugly, satisfied with Tom's mild obeisance, and sank back down in their chairs with choreographic unison.

"Tom," droned the spokesman, "it will please you to know that for weeks you have been our first choice for the new hotel position. We felt compelled to interview everyone. We couldn't very well place your interview first or near the beginning as everyone would have resented being put through a staging ordeal, so we slotted you next to last. We have, as you know, only Tony waiting outside. Now what do you say to 'Live '87, Be '87'? The announcement is set for the business news section of our local paper first thing in the morning. Just a phone call away."

He laughed hollowly, sending a smattering of obliging titter chain-reacting around the table. The spokesman then flagellated his soft hand as a shillelagh on the top of the conference table and launched a screeching chant, as nerve-shattering as chalk dragged down a blackboard — "Live '87,

Be '87"—. The other five clones of establishment gendarmerie recanted the slogan nineteen times — one horrible time, they announced at its blessed conclusion, for each floor in the new hotel. It was awful.

The shrillness of their damned, "Live '87, Be '87" dictate, under which Tom had labored all summer, turning former friends into slinking, suspicious vestiges of former selves, jarred him, roughly boxed his ears, and he snapped flatly, "No."

The grand assemblage twittered again. All their heads questioned horizontally. One pudgy, wheezing executive reached jerkily for the water pitcher and spilled himself nearly half a glass.

"Fun's fun," croaked the spokesman timidly. "Uh, Tom, you've been formally offered the position," he solemnized. "Live '87 is you, Tom." He pulpitized his fingers in a bony steeple under his chin and awaited Tom's acceptance.

Tom rustled himself into a straight-backed position, stretching his sleeping spine from its daydreaming stupor.

"Yes, '87 is mine. January, February, March, April, May. . .," Tom drew out the words distinctly, as a moderator wording names drawn at a lottery would do over a microphone.

The seated brain trust slumped and gasped in dismay. Their knees bumped under the table, causing little ripples of earthquaking movement in every newly poured glass of water.

Tom continued. "June, July, August, September, October, November, December. They have no year, any year, '87 or any other. They stand for themselves."

The spokesman dismantled his steepled hands and dropped them loosely. The blood in his well-nourished face took a sabbatical leave, exiting below his collar.

"Tom, we're, well, we're simply nonplussed." He polled the

bewildered faces of the other five. "What a grievous mistake, my boy. Do you know what this means — the ramifications, I mean? Quite frankly, Tom, it's a slam to management. I ... we're simply stunned.

"Well, what will you do? Of course you know we all would do anything we could for you, but staying here ... well ... I ..."

Tom arose from the hot seat and addressed the group.

"Gentlemen, any one of the other four would be great — exactly what you want for that new position. Me? I didn't know until fifteen minutes ago, viewing those marvelous paintings outside, that I would be accepting a firm offer from a half-hearted letter inquiry I made this summer, from reading *Hotel and Motel News,* alone in the snack shop on break, while I was losing the companionship of the other four, since your rats-in-a-cage 'Live '87' malarkey was started."

"Paintings? And where, doing what, where?" they clamored as geese being fed.

"Managing a motel lodge in the mountains for an elderly, arthritic couple. There are tremendous, tremendous benefits."

"Benefits?" they interspersed with baffled incredulity. "More than our group plan? Preposterous!"

"Yes. January, February, March that kind of group plan." Tom shrugged. "Would explaining matter? You have taught me a great deal. I'll give proper notice with my resignation. No hard feelings on my end. I hope the same on yours."

Tom bowed politely, claiming eye contract briefly with each befuddled pair of eyes, then he backed toward the paneled doors.

"Can I thank you for one more thing?" he asked, pausing, with one hand resting on the elegant door knob.

The little group sat mutely, round-shouldered, more shocked than affronted. Their thoroughbred racehorse hadn't placed! They watched him earnestly, a circle of wrinkled foreheads and narrowed eyelids.

"This painting exhibit out there on the balcony — your support of the arts. Civic-minded, indeed. Marvelous! Thanks so very much. It was priceless beyond words. By chance, have any of you viewed the paintings?"

No one spoke. Everyone at the table gazed perplexedly at one another, missing any nuance Tom was casting in their direction. Shutting the door behind him, Tom nodded a final thank you, audibly devoid of sarcastic overtone.

Pens were unclasped from shirt pockets and rapped moodily on the conference table top. The water pitcher clunked with usage. Two of the steaming executives loosened the top button on their shirts and slid their tie knots down a patrician inch. Their sighs were deafening.

The spokesman shuffled wistfully over to the conference room window, which overlooked the main entrance below where the steady stream of silver buses had nudged and hissed all summer. He parted the heavy, pleated drape for a moment, then let it flutter back to rest through parted fingers.

Unsummoned as yet, Tony, with the shock of Tom's sudden departure, was going mad out on the balcony. Little curls of fingernail, clipped by scissoring teeth, were piling up on the carpet. Tony was scooting them back under the bench with furtive employ of brooming foot.

"He was our first choice. Just incredible," bemoaned one of their number, now numb with mental paralysis, slumped about the astonished horseshoe of near circle, inside the chilly tomb of conference room. No reply ensued.

The spokesman still stood by the window. His coated back faced the conference table. He rustled the drape again, melancholically, and replied omnisciently, somewhat detached from supposed character.

"He was ours. We, not his. The laugh is on us. I'm afraid, gentlemen, that he knows some things we do not know. And, what is more ... we may never know them."

Cracking ice in the sweating pitcher broke the stony silence in the room.

NO COUNTS

"Can't see a thing, can you?" pestered Manley, peering up annoyingly at Milford, his somewhat taller companion. Manley flopped his soft, visored cap into an agitated and gloved hand, and swung his balding head fretfully, left then right. Unable to see the minister at the graveside before them, he was able only to hear the eulogy, spoken sing-songedly for their old, departed master. It was recited from somewhere within the close-shouldered stand of elegant winter coats, which surrounded the neat, rectangular cavity of earth.

"No much at all," tiptoed Milford, craning an icicle of ear to the ministerial drone, tolled for the huddled throng, which had gathered somewhat indignantly this shivering March to pay their last respects.

"He meant more to us than he did to them," asserted Manley, unhappy with their peripheral positioning at the family crypt, assigned there earlier by the robotic, blue-serged henchmen from the funeral parlor. Everyone had been decreed snooty, concentric circles of pecking order importance, radiating out from the open gravesite.

"And all of us to him in return," avowed Milford wistfully, speaking as embassy for the hired-help assemblage of six who were employing their handkerchiefs earnestly, with far greater blot of tearful urgency than the entire stand of prune-faced notables in front seemed to need, stamping about on the crunching crust of ground, deaf to the Scriptures, all trussed up to their sleek jowls in black and gray overcoats.

The octogenarian master had slipped away in bitter March, with a winter chill of his own, wasting away defiantly to the end, despite the battalion of nurses and doctors in his attendance, a myriad of umbilical connectors from glowing, mechanical carts, and purring medical computers rolled madly about in his mansioned, hospital bedroom.

A widower, since losing his lacy, young bride in the 1919 influenza epidemic, the old master had amassed a huge fortune between the two great World Wars, supplying molybdenum and magnesium for the infant aircraft industry. Never remarrying, he had lived out his life quietly on a baronial estate, dividing his time between abiding philatelic and numismatic romances, sequestered from the bustling metropolis which pulsated raucously only scant miles from his private hermitage.

He had patroned the arts anonymously during his lifetime and had given secretly by mail each day a $1,000 gift to some plighted soul, suffering somewhere across the nation. His hobby, other than stamps and coins, was prowling through out-of-town newspapers, discovering each afternoon at his ornate, pigeon-holed desk, the appropriate tragedy for his daily posted check of salve.

At the conclusion of the funeral ceremony, the cold-chattered little band of hired help scurried off. Manley had driven all of them in one of the limousines, parking it at the end of the processional queue, disguised behind thick, green shrubbery. Since the death of the old master four days earlier, no one had appeared to detail to any of the six any abrupt changes in normal routine, so Manley had meekly driven them all to the funeral, hopeful that continued use of one of the four limousines would not run any of them afoul with stern, surviving relatives, this grand-coated contingent frosting briefly about the graveside, separating in little knots of straightlaced urbanity to ponder the future dispensation of the old master's wealth.

Shepherded by Milford, the incongruous six faithfuls stooped into the limousine. They were, however, incongruous only to the antiseptic crowd at graveside, their pedigreed antithesis, not incongruous to the old master, as he, throughout his later years, bent on his cane-poked, creaking rounds about the estate, had visited daily each one at their duties. Unassuming, compassionate equality was always his human calling card.

Luisa, the Slovakian cook, rumbled in beside Manley and gasped to a rocking collapse. Buxom, beet of face, with blonde hair pin-cushioned in a tidy bun, she wore a closet of mismatched sweaters and shawls. Coatless by choice, her long blonde hair, if loosened, could have cascaded down to protect her bare neck. Her woven wrap of bun, however, a habit from cooking necessity, remained stoically up, as no insulator of natural stole against the biting cold.

Counterbalancing Luisa's stoutness in the front seat with his scabbard thinness, the old master's butler and valet, Wilson, unfolded his gaunt angularity beside her. Looking colder than the other five, the raw wind whipped his pencil legs. His straight, white hair bristled at his starched collar, giving it an unruly illusion. Uncomfortable in crowds, his prominent Adam's apply bobbed like the bubble in a carpenter's level. Seated in the limousine, each elbow and knee was a poised, sharp knife.

Milford held one of the rear doors open for Margaret, the

old master's housekeeper. She weaved sobbingly to a deep-cushioned seat, as a whipped flag in a gale. Her wispy, bony frailness battled thick mattresses at the mansion when they needed turning. Those assembled on breaks from routine to sip Luisa's steaming coffee, in the little room off the kitchen, could often hear her struggling above them, cursing as she toppled a cartwheeling mattress to a temporary rest on the floor.

Margaret and Luisa sustained the only occasional jealousy among the six. The old master had sensed this slight friction between them and had coaxed them both to share a shaky armistice. They had managed, and only occasionally were real bullets ever fired again. Margaret, it seemed, loved chocolates, and on her humming rounds she persisted in plopping them into her mouth from their perpetual bulge within a deep pocket in her pale yellow, rayon work blouse. Luisa loved chocolates, too, but gained weight, alas, by simply gazing at stalks of celery.

Along the rear seat, next to Margaret, slid Percy, the gardener. He stopped a full foot from her, and had to be goaded to slide on across so that room could be made for Milford. Percy was self-conscious about his perspiration, working outdoors with plants and flowers, and it didn't help his edginess when Luisa reminded him of his gamy aroma when he came around for coffee. Percy therefore shied from close proximity with people, even when he sported his Sunday best as he had this day for the old master's funeral. He sat quietly, exploring tiny rivers of rich earth in his cracked hands, rivers remaining beyond vigorous tussles with harsh, pumiceous soap. Percy, a horticultural wizard, could grow flowers up through solid concrete, but he was too modest and shy for anyone to know.

Milford, fiftyish, the ubiquitous handyman at the great estate, shut the door gingerly against his legs, as Percy had scooted over only half the distance he had been told. Orphaned, like Manley, he had come to live as a teenager at the great estate. An Edison with wiring and lanterns, a Carrier with airconditioning, and a Crane with plumbing, Milford, the exact body size of the old master, had become his close confidant over the many years. Through Milford, as the old master's mouthpiece, thoughts and suggestions from the kind benefactor had been communicated to the other five.

The old master had noticed Milford's natural intelligence when he was quite young. For many years, scrubbed after his duties, he had been permitted to scale the sliding ladder in the library to pluck great works of literature from the high shelves. These he devoured patiently with the old master's guidance assisting his quest for knowledge.

Milford, self-taught, had been proud to explain molybdenum and magnesium to Manley, in response to the chauffeur's broodings about the old master's life and fortune. Milford had simply looked them up in the musty, calfbound books in the library.

Among his assigned chores, Milford arranged each day the great stack of newspapers on the huge desk in the study — the source for the old master's daily, anonymous gifts. Wilson always felt that this duty fell squarely within the ambit of his valet and butler duties, but one haughty spat with Milford never graduated to picky pouting over chocolates, the childish variety of feud jousted between Luisa and Margaret on infrequent, steamy occasions.

After surveying the seated readiness of his five passengers,

Manley swiveled down behind the steering wheel and sparked the burly engine to life. Equatored like a top, he always puttered about the garage on the estate in a vest-buttoned chocolate brown sweater and baggy, rayon pants. The pants were nondescript mauve-brown, but in the sun, when Manley pulled the long cars out to hose them off, they cast a sheen of hideous purple. In the shade, when the precise machines were rolled back for their waxing massage, his rayon pants were passable, as grumpy slapdash allowance with his chocolate brown sweater, which had affixed itself perennially to his back as algae to a rock. At his master's funeral, he had buttoned himself to his chubby throat in his purple-gray uniform, save for his visored cap which had spent more time crumpled in his hand, largely through annoyance with their snubbed positioning at the funeral.

* * *

During the next few days the mansion seemed deserted, hollowly empty without its master. The six in its custodial care passed those tortoise days grieving their loss and sharing concern over their future. A few people stopped by, ostensibly relatives of the old master. They clomped through the quiet halls with the arrogance of conquering generals swaggering through subjugated cities.

Their children, starched in fashion plate correctness, visited real childhood, swinging down banisters and playing hide-and-seek behind the paneled doors. Their parents squeezed off rolls of celluloid, ignoring the half-dozen caretakers, who were there to be helpful if ever asked. Then undisclosing their departure to match their rudeness in arriving unannounced, the visitors would churn from the oval driveway, never pausing at the iron, front gate, sending sprays of loose gravel clunking into Percy's flower beds.

No authority of any type or description came out to the mansion to advise or counsel them during these lengthy, awkward days. Luisa made trays of burned croissants, politely avoided by all. Margaret had wanted to remark about them, but instead took a double dosage of chocolate as a tongue depressor. She changed bed linens forgetfully and fell down with mattresses flipped over only days earlier. Manley swirled the fenders of the big Lincoln until they needed painting. Wilson, his throat bobbing as a confused elevator, dusted shellac off newel posts and banisters.

Milford confided to Manley over Luisa's steaming coffee at their table off the kitchen that he felt certain he had heard Percy's clippers clacking away on shrubbery at three o'clock in the morning. Only Milford displayed normalcy with his actions, devouring the newspapers and sailing along on the wooden ladder in the library, thinking, thinking, while the others busied themselves with routine chores, unsettled about their future fate.

One afternoon, three weeks after the old master's funeral, a long sedan from the city loped around the circular driveway and stopped between the two statues of stern lion, which guarded the front staircase. This sedan was not, however, piloted by another of the old master's relatives popping out to ogle and covet the grandeur of the great estate.

"Thaddeus Breckinridge, representing the deceased's estate," the ruddy man announced to pallid Wilson at the front door, clutching his voluminous briefcase against his ample tummy with both arms so he wouldn't have to shake Wilson's taloned hand.

"Can you assemble everyone? I have important news from

the reading of the deceased's will that concerns all of you."
Wilson pistoned his throat and earth-gobbled off on his
rickety stilts to collect the group. Manley and Percy, from their
undemanding duties, crunched around the oval driveway from
opposite directions. Luisa shut off the wrong burner on the
stove, and teary-eyed, amid a cloud of escaping steam, summoned Milford from his mountain of newspaper reading at
the table in their little nook. Margaret floated diaphanously
down the main staircase when Wilson tugged the long, braided
sash.

When the group gathered uneasily in a cluster for mutual
protection in the drawing room, bloated Thaddeus
Breckinridge shuffled through his briefcase, straining the cliff-
edged anxiety of the moment.

"Well," he began condescendingly, "I have good news for
all of you." He waited pompously for a rejoiner of praise, which
totally failed to erupt across the confused faces of the group.
Missing his moment, he cleared his throat and retracted his
moated middle to a general curve of roundness at his beltline.

"It seems," he continued, "that all of you are provided for
very nicely. This estate is yours for life, indivisible for the six
of you, and, in addition, you each have a modest stipend each
year for the rest of your lives."

Breckinridge's glasses practically fogged over with misting,
greenish envy. He surveyed the elaborate, vaulted ceiling in the
drawing room, blinked at the dazzling chandeliers, and inspected over the bridge of his nose the Persian rug on which
they all stood. He then sighed mightily with mental indigestion
upon examining individually the hodgepodge of second-class
citizenry standing quietly before him in somber incredulity.

"It seems, also," he droned, "that the relatives are allowed to visit here no more than one week at any time. The deceased stipulated that the entire estate exists first for all of you, and only secondarily for any relatives, who may come for only short stays."

Breckinridge shook his jiggling cheeks and appeared on the verge of tears as if he had wolfed down a platter of tainted fish.

"No more than one week at a time," he murmured reluctantly.

Wilson and Margaret glanced sideways at each other and managed weak smiles. They swung their dual gaze beyond the open drawing room doors and pictured in the eye of their mind the staircase banister which would now groan and creak with sliding, yelping Indians only a blessed week at a time.

The portent of the good news also began to register with Luisa. She folded her massive forearms across her beefy middle the way she customarily delighted when her five cohorts moaned happily over one of her sumptuous meals. She didn't even leer at Margaret when she plunked a luscious cube of chocolate in her nervous mouth.

Manley brushed his omnipresent brown vest-sweater and twirled his chauffeur's cap on his forefinger. Percy bared timidly the full length of his jagged teeth. This was the closest facsimile to a smile Percy could muster. Silently he picked at earthen routes of darkness in his cracked hands. Milford rested his chin in a crotch of thumb and forefingers, and eulogized his old master to the assemblage with tribute of his own, delivered three weeks nearly to the hour, after the wintry day at the cemetery.

"He cared for us. I knew it would work out, even when we were herded like cattle to the rear at the funeral."

Breckinridge appeared almost ill, within easy earshot of

Milford's spontaneous soliloquy. He straightened his spectacles, crooked now across his nose, clasped his briefcase with papers protruding raggedly, and summarized his perfunctory duty. "Details will be forthcoming from my office. Good day to you all."

* * *

The months skipped along. Spring tempted bleak Winter from the land with sweet, waving wands of promise. Summer's hot breath strutted along, sharing alternatively for a time its warm days with the reluctant cool evenings of spring. Soon summer evicted spring, forcing it to pack and leave hurriedly, shouting it out with slaps of thunder. Then summer snoozed lazily on the front porch of the land, its domain won brutishly for itself.

A few nostril-elevated relatives pranced in to visit, but they left before staying a full week, knowing the rules and perishing the thought of being reminded by any servant of the old master's edict. None of the hired help would have dreamed of pulling rank in reciting the rules. They would have been too busy trying to make those royal visits pleasant for such an impoliteness to occur, but the foppish guests never considered that, too busy instead were they in avoiding any possible citation of calendar from lowly hired help, to even relax and enjoy themselves for a single day.

The newness and novelty of vacationing at the estate wore thin in a few short months, and by late summer the appointment calendar in Luisa's kitchen became more bare than shaded, with marked off days for arriving guests becoming fewer and fewer.

Milford grew restless, thoughtful, unsettled about things he couldn't quite pinpoint. He walked about the grounds at all hours. He read a great deal — local newspapers and passages from heavy, wine-red treatises in the library. Every faucet, every lamp, every fuse box, every pipe had been checked and rechecked. Time hung heavy with Milford's quick nimble mind. Hauntingly, he still brooded about the old master's funeral. The flame of autumn cracked across the mansion's grand driveway. Russet and gold leaves, orphaned by trees, scrunched in the wind, dying in glorious color, swirling bravely in dizzy tornadoes of rage with their last breath.

Painfully thin Margaret had ceased turning mattresses, and had alarmingly gained fourteen ounces with her chocolate consumption up nearly two boxes a month. Percy had haircut the shrubbery with military school abandon, shorter than ever before in his long tenure. He had then hidden his shears in horror, fearing he would denude the entire estate and be out of a job.

Wilson had moved the last of the old master's fine clothes down to Milford's apartment. The remainder of the instructions in the will from Mr. Breckinridge's office, delivered by a sophomoric law clerk on his lunch hour, had revealed a gift of the master's fine clothes to Milford, his exact double in size.

Manley had the fine cars, all four of them, so spankingly clean that he hated even to move them over the gravel driveway. Luisa had settled down in the kitchen to the calming point that petroleum jelly was scarcely ever needed for burns on her fleshy hands and arms. Earlier in the year, she had burned herself repeatedly, first from nervousness over their plight with the old master's passing, then with anxious concern over entertaining visiting relatives.

Milford marched about the spacious grounds with his hands Lincolnesque, folded behind his back, much in the manner of the old master before his cane became his walking neces-sity. On Milford's rounds, Percy, kneeling in the flower beds, would grin speechlessly, suggesting a simpleton friendship telegraphed only by his shyness. Milford observed the grow-ing lassitude of his little group. He sensed that they should be doing something, anything, to repay the old master for their lifelong allowance and the grandiose roof over their heads.

* * *

One wind-raked autumn afternoon, an early harbinger of that bitterly cold March day at the old master's funeral, Milford fairly shouted with exuberance. He urged Percy and Manley up to the house from the steps of the mansion. They shuffled around the gravel path, arcing from different direc-tions as they had the day Mr. Breckinridge came out with his good news. Margaret came down hastily, employing with rare usage, the clanking elevator. Wilson fetched Luisa, elbow-deep in dough, and the little band filed behind Milford into their room off the kitchen with a collective quizzical expression of caution, as if Mr. Breckinridge were back to explain a grievous error in his earlier announcements.

Milford blurted out his news before everyone was comfor-tably seated. Luisa pantingly tried to rise to perk a pot of cof-fee, but Milford guided her back down to a plopping seat.

"Remember the old master's funeral?" he hardly paused for a response. Margaret began to sob.

"I knew it wouldn't last," she said with quaking voice.

"No, no," reassured Milford, "I have no bad news. There's nothing to worry about. Remember the funeral, being pushed to the rear by those funeral parlor thugs, scooting us where to go with those outstretched arms and those false smiles?"

The seated five, even undemonstrative Percy, nodded ruefully with remembrance.

"It occurred to me, boom, like that," exploded Milford, smacking an open palm to his forehead, "that we all have the time and the ability, if we pinch a little, to brighten up funerals for folks like us — people thought to be "no counts" going to "no-count" funerals for people they loved.

The table was silent. Everyone sat rigidly with expressions of vagueness blind drawn to their chins.

"I've worked it all out," resumed Milford evangelically. "Walking the grounds these last few weeks, with time hanging on me, with everything fixed around here, it came to me. It looks like we won't be entertaining much. If they don't come in summer, they aren't coming."

Milford pushed back his chair and stood among them at the table.

"Listen to this. The old master would approve. With us using what we have, 'ingenuity,' he called it when we used to sit and talk on the back steps when he came around, we can pass on some happiness. Some of us, or all if we want, can attend funerals, some can prepare food baskets for wakes, some can cut flowers for wreaths, and some of us can deliver them, making people feel good with a big, shiny car coming around."

Luisa propped both arms aslant up on the table and pressed her doughy hands to her florid cheeks.

"I don't want no part of bein' irreveran' around the dear departed. It just ain't fittin'."

"I thought of that," Milford reassured her. "I have it all worked out. We'll attend funerals for those who pass on after long illnesses, poor people, down and out folks, people who won't have much of a funeral anyhow. I'll personally check the news in the local papers and watch it against the obituaries, and if a funeral is related to a sudden tragedy in any way, we won't go."

Luisa ruffled her skirt with appeasement, and returned her hands to an interlocking steeple on top of the table.

"We'll only go to those funerals where our presence with flowers, food, and Manley driving us in one of the big cars will uplift those who remain behind, letting them think that their dear departed was perhaps a little more important than they actually were."

Manley raised his arm as a child does in school, wishing to visit the restroom.

"Me?" he stammered queasily.

"Yes, you in your chauffeuring best, driving us around to funerals. Don't worry. The old master would approve. You'll see."

Milford detailed the whole operation, which he had envisioned so clearly while walking the grounds, itching with unsettledness and boredom. When he concluded, the little band of five, sufficiently donut-dunked with religiosity, stonily sat for a time, bewildered, huddling blankly over Luisa's newly arriving coffee.

Nearly an hour later, with only guarded curiosity, they slid their chairs back scratchily from the table and drifted off separately to their undemanding chores with Milford's enthusiastic rhetoric rattling around in their perplexed craniums.

Milford was not dissuaded by their mild reluctance. He had planted the seeds well. He plunged ahead excitedly the following week by pinning a large wall map of the city and its environs to the blank, windowless wall of their coffee nook. He placed a topless cigarbox filled with multi-colored pins as a centerpiece on their table.

The first day the map was up, the other five drifted by all day, scanning it from top to bottom like yokels musing impassionately over cubistic art in some great city museum. They noticed the large black X in the top left, suburban corner, highlighted by Milford's crayoned wording of, *WE ARE HERE.*

Manley asked Milford at supper that evening what the seven blue-capped pins meant, those pricked about the map after the large X was first drawn upon it.

"Those, my chauffeur extraordinaire, stand for our local cemeteries," he replied soothingly, placing a reassuring hand upon Manley's chocolate brown shoulder. Manley slumped sheepishly beneath Milford's friendly pat.

The next morning, at breakfast, Margaret wondered aloud about the nine red-capped pins which had mushroomed randomly into view since the previous evening.

"My exceptional housekeeper," Milford explained glowingly, "You're about to spread a little sunlight in your wonderful, charming manner and should be told that those nine pins represent funeral homes in this fair city of ours."

Margaret, wide-eyed with Milford's new vivacity, grumbled a reply and popped a chocolate in her mouth as panacea for the disease of having no further questions.

Without canvas chair and beret, Milford, nevertheless, became a Hollywood director about the mansion. Never dictatorially, but rather sweetly, persuasively, contagiously, he clapped his hands for action, dispatching little errands, while deaf and blind to their continuing mild reluctance and petty complaints about his grandiose plan.

Manley was sent into the city to secure four, shiny metallic plates for the front of each of the four limousines — plates scrolled with the initials of the master, JBT. On her weekly, Tuesday afternoon excursions to a theater matinee, a routine unbroken in a skein of 243 consecutive Tuesdays, Margaret was asked to drop by a nearby printing establishment to order little note cards and envelopes, similarly embossed with the initials JBT.

Milford wanted to tribute the old master with his plan. Using his actual initials, he felt, accomplished that. With the old master spending the last thirty years of his life in virtual obscurity, save very rare liaisons with a smattering of the black and gray coated princelings who shivered at his funeral, Milford advised the little group that JBT, when noticed, would never be traced back to their clandestine way of life at the mansion.

Wilson, on his off duty, Thursday afternoon, was given a chore list of stationery supplies to purchase. Manley drove him into town and circled the block seven times as Wilson labored over selections of posterboard, marking pencils, a new pair of scissors, scotch tape, and paper clips. His throat gobbled everywhere. Wilson was not accustomed to shopping. Luisa and Margaret had done all the shopping for years, in separate stores now, after once meeting by surprise at a confectionery counter in one store and engaging in pyrotechnics on the spot.

For all of these early expenditures, Milford, table-setting his plan for the others, hopeful they would come to his banquet, dipped conspicuously into his own pocket to pay for the necessary supplies. Wisely, he knew that his scheme needed the cooperation of all to be successful and that setting the right example could spur the contagion for it that he so earnestly hoped would germinate among them.

Percy slunk in one morning and rapped lightly at the doorway to Milford's command post, their cozy coffee nook. Milford laughed at his formality and beckoned him to enter, setting aside the local news section of the morning paper that he was coordinating, for drill, with the daily obituaries. Percy entered with Luisa's great bulk darkening the doorway behind him.

"Me and Luisa was talking." He looked down at his hands, then hid both black-rivered paws behind his back. "We was saying, he continued, "me, I could grow a garden, plenty room out back, and spend a little more time bringin' flowers around to bloom, for bouquets and all, for them poor departed's friends. I got the time with them shrubs cut back real good."

Luisa interrupted. "If Percy grows vegetables, too, what he's saying is, I can use them for us, at our table, for the six of us, and free up some allowance money for Percy and me to help with . . . uh, these bills of ours, I mean, yours, like you been doing, for giving no counts a lift like."

"That's great," Milford said. "That will help, and Luisa . . ." Milford paused and soothed a genuine thank you. "You said ours without thinking a moment ago. Wonderful! That's what this is, ours — our appreciation for what little we can do where it might do some good, like the old master's concern for us."

"Humph," retorted Luisa, more red-faced than usual. She thumped out mumbling, "I've something on the stove," leaving the newly proclaimed vegetable gardener alone with Milford.

In a few days, universal anticipation was flying high among the six as they prepared to attend their first funeral. Milford had become proficient at cataloguing obituaries with poor addresses on the large map. He judiciously separated obituaries resulting from tragedies and those describing the passing of well-to-do people. He knew that their presence at funerals for important people would go unnoticed and accomplish nothing, unlike that which he hoped to accomplish for the discouraged and downtrodden.

Goosebumped with anticipation, the day of their first funeral arrived. They were unrehearsed but very willing. Enthusiasm, won by Milford's persistent guile, had bolted fear. Manley had scouted the tiny, delapidated house in a poor section of the city the day before, thundering around in one of the four luxury vehicles, slowing appreciably for a windshield appraisal of the exact address, careful not to bump into trash barrels which littered the dirty street at both curbs.

Milford had cross-referenced the name in the obituary with the city directory, finding no address in the telephone book to match up with the name. Milford, in his early discoveries at his command post, had found few telephone listings for the very poor, and reasoned, quickly, that the very poor often lived without telephones, a fact which added to their insularity as lonely people.

On their maiden flight that day, Wilson suited up in his best, starched butler raiment and rode over to the climate-beaten, little hovel the morning of the funeral with a groaning basket of pies, cakes, and sandwiches prepared by Luisa, a bouquet of flowers grown and arranged by Percy, and a little note on the JBT stationery, beautifully scrolled by Margaret.

Manley idled the purring limousine at the curbing and nervously flopped his cap about his lap. Wilson, laden with presents, hurried up the broken, concrete path to the front door and placed the offering tidily at the door. He sampled the paint-chipped doorbell, and hearing no sound, smartly rapped his bony knuckles at the peeling door frame before rattling back to Manley at the curbing. His prominent throat bobbed up and down furiously when Manley cursedly stalled the engine, thereby delaying their dashing exit.

At noon, Milford penguined himself into one of the old master's fine suits. With satin top hat and silver-tipped cane, he allowed Margaret and Luisa to brush and fuss over him in front of Wilson's foyer mirror. Stately and stiffly, he lowered himself into the plushness of the ebony Lincoln and beckoned to the hesitant, purple-and-grayed chauffeur beyond the glass partition to be off for a leisurely drive to cemetery number five, designated as such by the blue-tipped pin on their map.

Manley rolled to a silent stop fully seventy-five yards from the grave site. He went around, escorted Milford out, and led him to a polite positioning, erect alongside the sparkling limousine. Milford removed his top hat and held it motionlessly in the crook of a tailored arm as if he were posing for a portrait.

Only three people had gathered with the threadbare minister at the grave. The words were brief, then the tractor-hiding grave attendants attacked the open hole with their shiny spades flying, much sooner at the service's puny conclusion than Milford had recalled a similar group of lurking attendants scooping into action at the old master's funeral.

As the destitute little batch of three, accompanied by their minister, sadly departed to their rusty vehicle, Milford and Manley knew they had been seen. Collective, toothless grins swept over the initialing on the front plate of the limousine, undoubtedly matching explanation for Margaret's initialed note, and then full smiles erupted across their faces and they nodded. Milford nodded courteously back to them. Manley bit his lip and fought not to flop his cap aimlessly.

As weeks progressed, Milford refined all trail-by-error excursions to streamline their operation so that their allowance money could be maximized for food baskets and store-bought bouquets when the final, undisputed arrival of winter made Percy's horticultural wonders more difficult to produce. Manley scouted poor houses, with Wilson squiring baskets, on the first run, instead of wasting gasoline with Manley going out alone for an initial inspection. Sometimes Manley would report back to Milford that the neighborhood of the newly departed was too nice. Sometimes he would announce that too many comforters had gathered in well-to-do, late model vehicles for their own sunshine trip to mean anything.

In these instances, Milford would scratch off the intended funeral trip on the big tally posterboard at his command post. When a basket of food came back, undelivered in these cases, Luisa simply served the crust-clipped sandwiches as lunch for the six of them. Nothing was ever wasted. Wilting, ungiven bouquets brightened up Wilson's main hall credenza and their gathering table in the coffee nook.

Once Milford sent Manley out to Grandview Drive, thinking it was Grandview Street. The liquored wake at the mansion there on Grandview Drive was too grand indeed for any following cemetery visit. Milford noted his mistake for future reference, schooling himself quickly on the subject of address descriptions. Rich people apparently lived on drives; poor folks, he supposed on just streets.

Manley and Wilson visited nursing homes and missions for wayward souls. They visited rest homes, maintaining folks infirm with the disease of dispiritedness. Sometimes Margaret rode with them. Wilson came to ascend steps confidently, without stumbling, when he delivered their victuals of concern on their various rounds.

Manley no longer twisted his cap. He left it squarely on his head. Rocking chairs on porches swayed with nodding appreciation, and tongues, largely silent without much pride or hope, wagged from the rocking chairs. Glints of wide surprise flickered in tired, cloudy eyes when the spruced limousines parked for Wilson and Margaret, so they could troop up walkways laden with goodies for the tummy and the eye.

Never engaging anyone in conversation, never ostentatious with their presence, the congregation of funeral vigilantes, in part or as a group, attended over a hundred funerals within a forty mile radius from their cloaked mansion during the ensuing year.

Luisa almost always stayed home, bustling about with the food baskets. Margaret sometimes dressed in a wisp of black and went along, but usually she stayed back, too, painstakingly writing loving notes of anonymous bereavement on the initialed stationery. Margaret had given up a box of candy a month, and her consecutive Tuesday streak at the movies had stopped at 251. She was now driven downtown to her Tuesday matinee only every other week.

Occasionally Percy, with vigorous employ of abrasive soap, would lighten the dark rivers of soil in his cracked hands and suit up clumsily in his Sunday best to ride out to the cemetery in the back seat between Milford and Wilson. Percy never got out of the grand cars when Manley parked them decorously on the periphery of funeral proceedings, but inwardly warmed himself through the windows, inspecting from afar while seated the profusion of flowers adorning nearby tombstones.

* * *

Having deposited their basket of care at a rarely visited ghetto mission on a hot day early in their second summer, the group of six, together uncommonly as a full unit, hummed to a creeping stop at a remote cemetery, one somewhat weedy and refuse-blown, fully thirty miles across the city from their secluded mansion.

Eight or ten emaciated onlookers wilted at the grave in the broil of the sun. The meager service had not begun. They wore a kaleidoscope of faded color, clothes either too tight or too loose, clean and washed by the mission but mismatched and missized in their eventual wearing. They were all middle-aged, but appeared older. Their noses, roseolas of alcohol, beaconed prominently on skin-sagged faces. Their blue, paneled van, with the name of the mission fading in white, sat truantly near, as if not wanting any of its passengers very far from sight.

Mickey hoarsely grated to his gaunt companion, Ernie, "See 'em, here payin' 'spects to Tommy, all dolled up and lookin' fine?" Mickey, displaying his white gums, poked Ernie in his cage of ribs.

"Yup, Tommy had fine friends," winced Ernie, massaging his bony side with a smoke-yellowed clamp of thumb and forefinger.

"Why sure, musta. Look at 'em. You seen 'em at da mission this mornin', fancy card they passed 'round da porch with them purdy flowers."

"Kinda thought Tommy was oncet somebody," offered Ernie, hopeful his agreements with Mickey would preclude another elbow slug in the ribs.

"Clear as your face," ratified Mickey, elbowing Ernie again. "Them's fine folks, what knew Tommy. He was s-o-m-e-b-o-d-y, I betcha, always reading them newspapers and pamflets 'round da mission. We shoulda knowt. Kinda fills a body up, don't it, Ernie?"

"Yup, I'd like somebody fine coming to my funeral someday."

"Darn tootin'."

"That's for sure," mimicked Ernie, not knowing yet if answers or no answers were best insurance against emphatic elbow assaults.

"Say, tell you what, what say we make anotha' run of it?" spirited Mickey.

"Whatcha mean?"

"Say we make anotha' run at it — 'ployment, a job."

"Shucks, suits me." Ernie shrugged.

"I got one awaitin' me, clerkin'. Coun'selr' wants I should take it. You?" summoned Mickey.

"Got one too if I want it; just ain't said yes yet. Could easy 'nough."

"First thing tomorra then, what say? I'm tired of them headaches."

"Suits me. Sure, I don't mind trying again," declared Ernie.

"One thing for sure, we ain't gonna find no nice, 'pecial folks like Tommy knowt for comin' to our funeral, wastin' out days at dat mission. I'm apt ta really try this time. That Tommy now, he was SOMEBODY!"

SOUTH BY NORTHEAST

Not so very long ago, a little more than a brief decade in time, there existed, northeast by a dozen miles from the great city to its south, a hidden community. Its pioneering, remote isolation, in those days labeled astonishingly bold by many, was proud and self-reliant. Its sprawl of homes, sprinkled leisurely on acre-sized lots, was in rural, happy wedlock with nature. The dwellings elbow-roomed contentedly, devoid of any encompass of restraining brick walls or barricading security guardhouses, snooty stockades which seemed to coldly characterize fancy developments elsewhere.

The cozy community boasted an authentic Indian name which rolled off the tongue like syrup into a catch pail, the kind of sweet-sounding name that reminded one of magical places like Minnehaha and Gitche Gumee, in Longfellow's enchanting poem, *The Song of Hiawatha.*

The early homeowners in this sylvan glen northeast of the throbbing city were never smug about their good fortune in being able to live there. Their homes, on generous parcels of land, were not terribly exclusive, just apart enough, as stamps licked to large envelopes, to offer the distinct impression of supposed estate status without being estates in actuality.

Realistically, many families who lived there had two breadwinners, husband and wife scooting into the city each day to wrest a dual salary in that beehiving tumult. In those early days, going back to any store in town, once one was delightfully home, was a planned campaign in logistics. Equidistant at four miles, and in nearly exacting, opposite directions, were the four closest family markets where an overlooked loaf of bread or a forgotten gallon of milk could be collected on a sleepy Sunday morning.

The locations of the four stores were not exactly quartered out on the four equal parts of the compass, but practically so. The stores were scribed in the four basic directions: north, south, east, and west. The residents played no favorites. One store was four miles away like the other three, so they simply rotated their patronage, wanting all the stores to survive, as the residents were prairie generous in that way, neighborly and supportive, helping where they could be helpful, while ever guarding their individualistic privacy.

During those early days, tucked beyond the swirling nebula of city, barely safe from its ravenous, gravitational fury, country living was luxurious, languorous as a daydream, lazy as a leaf rafting down a quiet stream. The raucous clank of the city seemed far away, curtained off by the swishing draperies of cool, green trees. In those glorious times, whippoorwills returned each year to herald the arrival of Spring. Loafing cows in nearby pastures mooed softly in the deep night and along the meandering creeks, otters floated on their backs, whiskered as corpulent entrepreneurs in lavish swimming pools at fancy resorts.

Alligators in the little ponds cruised sullenly with bony ridges above their eyes and snouts peeking out as they glided. Only telltale bubbles signaled their departure when they had seen enough, deciding to vacate below whenever the curious, approaching stares of man ventured too close. Great herons highstepped in the watery grasses, swiveling their heads gracefully. Newspaper delivery men, on duty in the pink-gray of early morning, reported seeing wily foxes trotting on pencil legs across the roads, just at the ending power of their yellow headlights.

However, the bucolic charm of the residential preserve could not remain a guarded secret. Every perpendicular index finger figuratively pressed against sealed lips was snatched away rudely by invisible and grabby hands. The dream of remaining a secret was gossamer, cruelly impossible to clutch and hold dear. That precious notion could not be cached in any safe hiding place, or buried in a jar in the deep woods. The hushed fancy was discovered, then pursued and stalked avidly by all manner of people who would not idly let it be.

The quaint, serpentive coils of country road, which had nudged out there around the orange groves, pasture, and thicketed woodlots in the 1920's and 1930's were ideal for exploration — picturesque arteries already in place for land developers. They were perfect, those rustic country lanes, with their fanciful charm supplying, in and of themselves, the subliminal notion of snug country living. All the guileful developers had to do was slapdash together new housing gambits, checkmate them beyond thick, foreboding brick walls, dredge up different Indian names for their new monstrosities as further exotic enticement, then sit back retiringly, letting the weaving country lanes orchestrate the needed condiment of charm.

For the entire ensuing decade, the Ten Years War, battalions of construction workers camped out northeast of the great city, surrounding the defenseless, quiet community, as vast armies billeted on a high plain overlooking their object of siege.

In every direction, large tracts of orange grove and pasture were bulldozed, and white construction trailers were plopped upon the naked ground to oversee the planned carnage. Solitary oak trees, ribboned for safety, sometimes escaped the guillotine of bulldozer, their right to live proclaimed not by merciful compassion but so prospective purchasers of homes could point at them and giggle, "Oh! look, they have some trees."

In the mornings, when people drove to work, they began to leave their homes earlier and earlier each day.

Convenience stores mushroomed up overnight, closer by distance than the four original outposts of general store, the folksy mom-and-pop markets which had served so well. Strip shopping centers then swaggered out to the country to update the modern-day sodbusters to the glitzy reality of bustling city life, a reality from which they had hoped to be excused for a few hours each day. Well-meaning churches, splinter denominations with friendly, homey names, but without sound monetary budgets, ascended to skeletal roofs above concrete block modesty.

In the mornings, the people drove to work, leaving their homes earlier and earlier each year.

Shortly thereafter, the development companies waltzed a slick "two foot shuffle" at the residents, sneaking onto their stage a hastily drawn score for condominiums to be erected near the original nest of homes, a coded plan which attempted to rewrite the county density allotment for new construction. Just in the nick of time, the stunned residents banded as torchbearing vigilantes might gather at a town meeting, and successfully beat back the developer's scheme.

The seed for condominiums had been planted, however, and the seed would come to ingest hungrily the fertilizer generously applied by the developers. The seed would be nurtured again, and cultivated more scientifically than at its first planting when the developers had grinningly trotted out their Trojan horse, an original disguise of amateurish preparedness. The next time, they had their legal machinery of intent formed as a mighty phalanx across a broad front of paperwork propriety. The residents, with only hoes and rakes in their rhetorical arsenal, were driven back to sulk in their homes. The developers controlled the meetings.

Backyard prattle turned away from nagging crabgrass, the best choice in barbeque briquets, the care of children's teeth, and the outcome of the major league baseball season, to focus directly on each person's modus operandi for simply getting to work in the mornings. Power lawnmowers roared in marked time neutral while sweaty neighbors debated this route and that route.

Philantropic neighbors offered suggestions and advice, and occasionally even the ultimate in honorable, golden rule neighborliness, the open divulgence of a special route which had saved time for them. The covetous, self-serving neighbors were polite enough, shrugging privately that magnanimity was certainly laudatory, but the telling of any secret way to the great city to the south was dangerous, good for the ears of a backyard neighbor, but how could a soul be sure that the telling of a secret route wouldn't be blabbed to others. One could not be too careful. At stake was something momentous, the fight to get to work.

In the dark mornings, long lines of red tail lights, ruby-paste necklaces cast upon the boudoir dresser of gaudy opulence, streamed out in every direction, like dizzy spokes in an ever-revolving wheel.

Schools appeared magically along the country lanes. Police were soon summoned to usher fleets of buses during peak arrival and departure times. A nearby high school, its growth spurred by the burgeoning state university close to it, became the largest high school in the area. Children drove their cars nine miles to get to this school, in a huge roundabout loop from another direction, in order to combat the pestering traffic. The more direct route, snarled by bumper-riding vehicles, was only six miles in distance from their homes. New traffic signals swung in the breeze over busy crossings, where, only short years beforehand rattling armadillos and poky turtles had confidently and fearlessly crossed the country lanes.

And the people drove to work in the mornings, leaving their homes earlier and earlier each year.

People who lived on the main country lanes turned their cars around in the driveways at night, facing them out toward the next morning's zipping adventure in order to improve their chances of scooting out onto the morning conveyor without getting crunched from the other direction. Quiet residential streets near traffic signals became thoroughfares as people shot through them, cutting a mischievous, diagonal route across the nudging snarl, hopeful to gain precious time on their fellow motorists.

The shoulders of roads became roads themselves, lacking only true pavement and painted lines, as people passed inching cars on the right, billowing clouds of dust in their lurching, bumping scramble to save time. People glared, assaulted their horns, and whitened their knuckles on their steering wheels. Motorists who were normally polite became brutalized by the choking congestion, jabbing fingers rudely in the air at other drivers, demanding to be allowed to butt up in line rather than gesturing inquiringly for the favor.

The stop-and-start routine at road construction sites, slaving under everywhere to swiveling "orange-means-slow" and "red-means-stop" signs, became a way of life — a reluctant barter for survival. Coaxingly, people hung out their driverside doors to beg early passage, even unfolding themselves from behind the wheel to fidget and fume by their car fenders, shielding their eyes in the sun while craning for a better view up ahead. They cajoled yawning attendants with sugary pleas in attempts to have their stopped line awarded rapid resumption of movement.

The little bridges, built decades earlier to span the snaking creeks, groaned beneath the exponential increase in vehicular traffic. They creaked and trembled. County officials and civilian engineers drove out to look and to ponder, scratching their damp foreheads under sweaty ballcaps, while cogitating with shoots of grass sawing between spaces in their teeth. They peered and poked, then poked and peered, remaining largely silent, their inadvertent answer for a dilemma that was fast becoming unanswerable.

The greatest agony of all occurred when the dazed people queued up in their cars in the morning darkness along the country lanes. As they snailed along, they had ample time to gaze moodily out their windows. Homes were under construction in every conceivable direction. At the construction sites, on winter mornings before the workday began, work crews huddled around fires, and on summer mornings, the crews shaded about the gargantuan machines, dripping their first perspiration of the day in the quick humidity of slanting early morning. The city-bound gnomes eyed the construction workers warily. The construction workers stared stonily back at the motorists.

Hatfields and McCoys!

The people knew they were trapped, and would be trapped for years to come. The labyrinth of new construction would ooze out onto the country lanes for years before anything could be done about the connecting roads. Spillage of new motorists mixing onto the roads from new developments was a dizzy overlay for every county map in existence. New neighborhoods took only six months or less to breathe life, but completion of new, adequate roads would take years.

The people closed up the long lines every darkened morning with accelerator spurts of a few feet at a time, and were forced to view their own executions, scaffolded about them by hammer and saw as they watched, trapped there with no further appeal to be heard.

The horror of all motoring horrors then occurred. The main bridge to the jobs in the south, the bridge near the university which crossed the only legitimate river along the network of limpid creeks, was sagging, weakened from the onslaught of a decade of bombarding pummel by weighty construction trucks.

The people panicked. Burly police kept a vigil at the bridge, warding off lumbering trucks until decisions could be made. Rumors ran rampant while people poured over county maps, as generals in advancing battle, trying to devise a new way to get to work if indeed the bridge had to undergo surgical repairs.

The officials adjudicated the bridge unsafe. The road was closed for weeks while crews scurried under the bridge, adding a stronger spine, as a hopeful bandaiding allowance for its continued use. The people prayed that no new bridge would be required, further complicating their harried lives.

During the repairs, they grumpily shopped downtown after work and rearranged their daily routine, spending less time at home. Anything was better than stumbling home bone-tired each night, befuddled by the invisible carbon monoxide fumes in the endless bumper chains, which were now slowed to a walking crawl by the hassle of bridge repairs.

The people sought capillary relief everywhere with the main artery now clogged in the form of a vital bridge closed for essential repairs. Early in the mornings, really in the dead of night, without any sliver of comforting pink in the eastern sky, the people drove northeast to go south, miles out of their way. They sped through tiny country hamlets which had never experienced such activity, past open pasture, arousing sleepy cows, and past dense wood forests, squashing nocturnal opossums and raccoons inadvertently with their humming tires.

Northeast they went, northeast by necessity, a baffling end run for the south.

The good people were tired before their workday really had a chance to begin.

And many, many good people—most, in fact—knew not why!

A MODERN HALLOWEEN

Rick trooped through the electronic doors of the supermarket, which hissed apart for him with metallic impersonality. He wove through the late afternoon shopping throng which bustled excitedly with the festive promise of the evening before them.

Cardboard goblins in orange and black decorated the front of the store. They stood stonily silent, as eerie museum figures, lifelike for a second glance, propped up in bins of hard rock candy and alongside pyramidal displays of bottled apple cider. A ghost, with facial features crayoned across an ordinary bedsheet, moved up and down threateningly, puppeted by a nearly invisible string.

Rick whisked down a far aisle to the fresh produce section at the rear of the store. With the time change the previous Sunday, only a little more than an hour of daylight remained until full darkness, and full darkness usually meant early arriving "trick-or-treaters," so Rick was brisk with his hurry along the tiled corridor. He had wanted to purchase a pumpkin at the roadside stand as he had normally done each year, but he hadn't seen any roadside pumpkins beckon that afternoon. Perhaps he had waited too long this year for success with that variety of natural, rustic pumpkin acquisition.

From a neat row on the floor, beneath the cafeteria counter of fresh vegetables, he picked up the first plump, basically round pumpkin he could find. He rotated it, searching for a good place to create a face. He made his choice after examining only three likely candidates, and was hastening to leave when the kindly lady in the homey apron and white dress, who tantalized cart-heaping shoppers with free, delicious tidbits at her small table, interpleaded.

"No, take the one with the stem for a lid." She smiled angelically, hopeful Rick wouldn't think her officious with her advice.

"H'mm." Rick smiled back at her. "Good idea."

He returned the one first selected to bondage on the floor and gathered another, one with a stem-like chapeau sprouting from its top. She nodded approvingly, and Rick thanked her for her thoughtfulness.

The express checkout lane was swift and merciful. Rick galloped out the separating doors, mentally tallying his preparation for major surgery on his pumpkin. There was a suitable candle in the pantry. He had checked that before leaving for work that morning. Hurrying to his car, he glanced fleetingly at the ball of red, aslant in the western sky, absconding now with its autumnal prisoner of cerulean blue, cloaked now in purple for its tethered passage into night.

He would have to hurry so that he could lumber through an evening jog in addition to the most pressing matter of readying the front of his home for masked and costumed children. He loosened his tie as he drove along, then huffily removed the chokecollar entirely and dropped it on the seat, next to his faceless pumpkin, which was soon to be anesthetized with coaxing words on his dining room table operatory.

Darting into his driveway, Rick cut his engine and scrambled madly through his home. He didn't even check for mail in the mailbox. He placed the pumpkin on the dining room table, then slung a handful of old, folded newspaper, retrieved nearby from a magazine rack, beside it. He rummaged through a kitchen drawer for a butcher knife, and located once again the battered-and-creased cardboard sorcerer, the family Vincent Price with fangs, which had reposed darkly for a year within the hall closet.

He returned to the dining room, forgetting the portable trash can. He muttered a curse to an empty house and bent to peer out the dining room window to chart the progress of the quickly setting sun.

"Darn it," he growled, "got to get a jog in." Stubbing his toe on a cloaked dining room table leg, he limped back to the kitchen for the trash can.

This year Rick would perform the pumpkin surgery. Usually, his wife discharged this duty, expertly giving the orange surface a toothed grin, notched eyes, and an isosceles triangle for a nose, all carved with deft swirl of paring knife. His wife was attending opera chorus practice, however, and wouldn't be home until late in the evening, so he was chief-surgeon-in-residence tonight. The costumed little tykes would have to settle for what he could do.

Rick wasn't about to try to emulate his wife's artistry with the blade. He cut an unsymmetrical lid off the top of the pumpkin and used the stem conveniently as a handle to set it wobbly aside. He then plunged his hand into the gooey, stringy brains of his scalped sphere.

"A surgeon I would never make," Rick declared to the dining room walls. He disemboweled the muted patient. He slung dripping gobs of seed off his fingers, in a damp trail across the spread newspapers. The pumpkin's smile was an uneven slash of a grin, totally devoid of notches for teeth. Rick had resigned that he wouldn't have fingers left if he had tried to cut teeth. Two, fairly neat pyramids, popped out with press of thumb from inside the cavity, served as eyes. Rick skipped the nose.

Folding and crumpling soggy newspaper for deposit into the trash can, Rick scooped up the pumpkin gingerly into the crook of one arm, retrieved the white candle from the pantry, picked up gaunt and ghastly Vincent Price, and loped out his front door.

He arranged Vincent on a trusty nail on the front door, the one which held cardboard turkeys, white Easter bunnies ribboned in pastel bunting, and holly wreaths, depending upon the monthly dictate of the calendar. He positioned the taloned hands in a clutching, threatening pose, then stood back to admire his handiwork as one admires a painting in a gallery that is supposed to be adored by all when it really appears to be horrid and inscrutable from every possible viewing angle.

He trotted around to the rear of the house and fetched a patio table for the pumpkin. Returning, he stole another furtive glance at the fading red ball in the sky, which was now beginning to flirt up the sleeve of a magician.

"Darn it," pined Rick, "I need to get a jog in."

Snapping his fingers to herald his forgetfulness, he hustled back inside the house for a box of matches, then applauded himself on the extra, time-consuming trip when he remembered the candy, thus avoiding another repetitious trip inside.

"That saved some time," he proclaimed. Outside again, he clattered into a large soup bowl, selected from its inaction under a kitchen counter, a Niagara of rock candy, spilled in loudly from two cellophane bags ripped open clumsily. He tucked the bowl behind his patio chair. Turning his chair slightly, he arranged his future seat so he could see completely up his driveway and still have a clear view of his flickering pumpkin. Rick then proceeded to flunk his Boy Scout merit badge exam. Two matches for a fire — they couldn't be serious. Rick started and extinguished nine matches before he could get enough wax from the candle to drip hotly inside the pumpkin cavity in order to form an adhesive base on which the candle could stand. He burned two fingers and watered his eyes before he could get the tottering bearer of flame to glow with a confined, faint sputter of light.

Finally he was finished with his preparation. Only his jog awaited, before the masked pilgrimage began to his little Halloween shrine. At least he hoped for a parade of little tykes, and the happy task of trying to guess their names and identities behind giggling masks. Rick furrowed his brow thoughtfully. The once steady stream of happy contagion to his front door had decreased dramatically in recent years.

"Surely they'll come," he pondered fortifyingly, proud with his readying efforts for their enjoyment and approval.

A sigh was a fugitive escaping past pouched cheeks as he stepped back to survey his twenty-minute blitzkrieg of preparedness. Glowing pumpkin, macabre Vincent, twinkling red and gold jewels of candy, and a correctly positioned patio chair were inspected and found to be ready. Rick saluted his four lieutenants as a general departs in the field after a final briefing, then galloped back through his front door to slip into his sweat-ripened jogging duds. He had started down the hall to his bedroom when he stopped abruptly and snapped his fingers annoyingly.

"Will I ever get organized?" he pleaded to the ceiling. With his wife at singing practice, his daughter at her boy friend's house, deciding to wait out the monster vigil there, and his son away at college, there was no one around to remind him of little details, as had been the case normally in past years when most family members had been home on Halloween evenings.

"Towel and a big, big Coke," Rick muttered. He pivoted in the hall and retraced his steps to the kitchen. There he drained a hissing, foaming Coke into a tall glass for a chilly swim with a tray of icecubes, and, balancing it carefully, yanked a thirsty towel from the stack atop the clothes dryer in the laundry room. He returned outside to hide the crackling soft drink behind his chair where he wouldn't inadvertantly bump it, then he positioned carefully the folded towel squarely atop the tall glass to ward off bugs until he could quaff his liquid reward at the merciful conclusion of his jog.

Once more with a wailing sigh, he hurried back through his front door, and this time knocked on the front porch lights. This was the one day of the year that the orange bug lights added appropriately to the color scheme of the holiday. Rick mused smugly to himself. He was pleased. Only his jog remained, and he had just enough time — twelve or fifteen minutes until full darkness conquered the fleeing day.

Holding his breath while he laboriously armored himself in his sweat clothes, Rick burst out his door like Dagwood Bumstead about to collide again with the mailman. The tiny flame in the pumpkin flickered in the wind vacuum of the slamming door. Rick coaxed it to a steady glow again, with tiptoeing passage and a perpendicular index finger pressed against pleading lips.

He chugged around his driveway. As he huffed around, his year-round coat of suet, never bulky anywhere, but lightly present everywhere, scended up and down. Mandrake had hidden the blood-red orb well up his sleeve. The last few laps of the twenty-one laps which measured a mile around Rick's driveway were waged as war against cardiorespiratory protestation, at the moment of day's final curtain. Rick briskly walked three more laps as a race horse is soothed by a morning handler after a spirited workout, then he padded to his front porch. He dumped himself into his chair, lassoed his soaking neck with compress of towel, and leaned back wearily.

With quivering voice, in squeaky, syllabic hyphens broken off between the last vestiges of jogging pant, Rick gave notice to all, "Anytime now, I'm ready."

The air was still and warm. It had been an unseasonably warm October, with no true arrival of autumn occurring anytime during the month. Rick rhythmized his recovering heart and lungs with slugging gulps of icy Coke. He swept the absorbent towel across his sopping brow and tingled with the afterglow of his run, refreshed from his busy day.

* * *

Fifteen minutes passed. Nothing happened. Twenty minutes passed. Nothing.

Rick nervously shifted his weight in his chair and glanced up at the fierce sorcerer. Vincent glared back at him mockingly, burning his ingot-eyes through the lambent glow of the candle. Rick looked away cowardly, and shuddered.

A full half-hour passed. Night had spaded down for a foxhole siege, but nothing happened. Rick thought he could hear the voices of children in the distance. He inclined a straining ear, and hoped he had heard correctly. He couldn't be sure. His mind was tricking him. He stole a peek at Vincent, transmogrified in the gloom, and waved a brave hand in his direction, laughing hollowly.

At forty minutes with still no arriving spooks, Rick stood up creakily and methodically fidgeted around his little shrine. Everything was in order — the pumpkin, the candy, the candle, cardboard Vincent. Any kid would come out okay, stopping by, with such a display to examine. Weren't they coming?

Rick went slowly back through his front door and slouched dejectedly into the kitchen to dial his parents at their apartment in the city, nine miles to the south.

"Hi, Dad, how goes it?" Rick asked when his dad answered.

"Fine, and with you?" came a guarded reply. His father wasn't accustomed to non-emergency calls at night.

"Fine, I guess. Say," blurted Rick, "I guess . . . guess you've had a lot of gremlins over your way, huh?"

"Not really," his father replied with a modest laugh.

"Really?" breathed Rick.

"Afraid so."

"Strange, isn't it?" ventured Rick, casting out topical bait.

"Pitiful is probably more accurate," saged his father.

"Yeah, pitiful," lamented Rick.

"Been headed that way for years now. Expect it one day just to end altogether, probably like man himself," philosophized his father.

A tomby silence ensued. Neither generation spoke. The twenty seconds of silence seemed as epochal as the entire Age of Reptiles.

Rick cautiously continued. "Had . . . many?"

His father laughed meekly.

"One."

"One?" Rick glimmered hopefully.

"If you can count it as one," wearied his father.

"Meaning?"

"Meaning the lady next door ... her grandson. They walked twenty feet and she right with him like those junior police guards when you were in grammar school."

"Oh!" Rick nodded into his receiver.

The phone call was agonizing. Rick struggled to salvage it. "Dad, tell me about the Bronx, in the twenties, when you went trick-or-treating."

His dad laughed.

"That's a long time ago."

"I know, but tell me. I'm interested."

"Well, you may not believe it," his father drew out wistfully.

"Go on, try me."

"Okay, you asked for it. Sure they had crime and thugs in the Bronx in the twenties when I was a kid, but we used to walk for miles at Halloween with never a problem. It was much darker in those days, with just lampposts. It never occurred to us that there was danger anywhere. Organized crime never touched kids. Shucks, their kids were out, too. And weird nuts? I grew up in the Bronx, but I don't know where they all were in my time ... we never heard of any. The biggest scare we ever got at Halloween was worrying about being chased by some shopkeeper after we soaped his windows.

"I bet it was great," fantisized Rick.

"You hit the nail on the head, son. It was great fun."

The two generations paused again on the wire.

Rick's dad resumed. "How many out your way?"

"Not one, so far," he reported solemnly.

"Well, maybe something will happen soon."

"Right, see you, Dad. Maybe you'll have some more over there."

Rick replaced the receiver thoughtfully. He slunk into the dining room and peeked around the curtains. Nothing. The driveway and walkway to his front door were devoid of human form trussed up in any manner of inhuman costuming. Rick released the curtains and allowed them to sway pendulously back to their silent rest.

He meandered into the family room and moodily switched on the television. The deep tunnel of gray gloom blinked awake. Rick, in hangdog grouse, slumped beside the brightness with his shoulders rounded forward. One free arm drooped defeatedly between his knees as he fumbled with the station slide bar with the other. It had now been a full hour since total darkness.

Rick witnessed a murder, saw a carload of thugs chased by police zoom off the end of a pier into a watery grave, broke in on a knife fight at some sawdust-floored roadhouse, and sympathized with a beautiful blonde in a light blue negligee as she banged for help on a barricaded bedroom door with her toneless, wall-ripped telephone dangling uselessly to the floor.

His hand settled on a channel with a narration about beautiful and colorful butterfly chrysalises. He sunk down in the deep armchair spent with the labor of changing channels from one violent episode to another. In this whirl of viewing selection, however, before staying with the intriguing program on larval and pupal stages in butterfly development, he had suffered through segments of two, horrid commercials extolling life in the fast lane and the way to create discriminating tastes for those on the way up.

"Up to where?" Rick had venomed aloud, rotating his head away from the nonsense prior to finding the blessed respite from violence with the nature programming on butterflies. For a few enchanting moments he was lost in the program, engrossed in the miraculous event, and he practically forgot the poor business state of free candy, floundering in near bankruptcy at his front door.

He bolted up refreshed and hurried outside again. The candle was only half its original height, and now the pumpkin revealed its glow through its sneering slash of mouth. The pyramidal eyes were nearly sightless. Rick squatted back down in his patio chair with renewing hope. His remaining Coke had married the last, eligible sliver of ice and they lived indivisibly as one, diluted and warmer.

He sat still, breathlessly, so that the sounds of night could sensate his consciousness. Desperately, he tried to chart neighborhood activity. His mind played tricks with him again. There must be a logical answer for no activity he sorted anxiously. He wanted an answer, so he invented one in his mind as cardboard flimsy as mad Vincent hung on the nail.

Sure, he concluded, the kids in our neighborhood are grown, like my two — too old now to venture forth this last day of October without getting laughed at by their peers. Rick slapped his thighs resoundingly through his drying sweatpants. How stupid! He palmed his forehead in mock self-punishment. Rick was almost elated.

Then realism returned, creeping back darkly to sing dulcetly to his pliant mind. He assembled the truth reluctantly in his mind. When he left for work in the mornings, the bus stops were just as large as ever with their knots of laughing, pushing kids. Families moved in and out of the neighborhood regularly, supplying new school-aged children on a random replacement basis for those growing too old for trick-or-treating. Rick felt worse that ever. He had felt good, briefly, relievably, with his flimsy sciolism, but he was forced to admit that his temporary clarity was full of gaping holes.

Faintly his right ear caught the unmistakable sound of young, playful laughter not two blocks away. Rick sat upright, brushed his jogging suit for non-existent lint, and ran his hand down through the rock candy, rearranging the cellophaned, crinkling jewels for luck, the way a carnival barker plays with loose change in his waist-encircling apron while sizing up new customers at his canvas booth.

The wait had been so long that Rick was a little nervous. He laughed aloud at himself and blushed at the notion of a proven salesperson in business, anxious over some cute, smear-faced kid tripping up to his door to stutter his practiced one line, "trick-or-treat, money or eats."

Rick heard their clatter grow louder. They were only a block away. He rose and craned his head through the trees to get a better view. An auto with two watchful yellow eyes, undoubtedly piloted by a father or mother, sputtered alongside the step of two children, matching their stubby gait with a coughing engine, which was struggling to keep itself going at the crawling pace. The auto neared the corner, close to Rick's driveway. Rick was panicky, as a sun-blistered man roasting in a rowboat panics, with his only shirt on a stick, madly trying to signal a passing, smoke-stacked freighter, indifferently puffing past on the distant horizon. With headlights illuminating his view, Rick spied one child robed in a bedsheet, tripping along, half falling over a trail of cloth; the other, with a chest of white bones, he could discern also, as the huddling mother hen of auto negotiated the corner at the pace of a funeral procession. His first, likely customers weren't even coming his way. They had turned up another street.

Rick picked up his empty glass and trudged back into the house. He freshened his drink in the kitchen and switched on the lamp by his favorite lounge chair in the family room. Plunking himself down, he stacked the morning newspaper, read earlier at break of day, once more atop his lap. He snatched at the movie page, crinkling it loudly in his disconsolate hands.

It was still fairly early, although full darkness was a full ninety minutes into its voyage for morning. Since his daughter and wife would be home late, Rick contemplated a movie to assuage his disappointment.

He clawed through the entertainment section, intent on finding something worthwhile to see, and anguished at what violated his eyes. The titles squirmed like snakes.

TO LIVE AND DIE   TARGET   FRIGHT NIGHT
ONCE BITTEN   ROCKY HORROR   DEATH WISH III
DAM OF THE DEAD   COMMANDO   LIVING DEAD

And then awash with unhappiness, the masterpiece of vomit, *TEXAS CHAIN SAW MASSACRE* raped his eyes.

He crumpled the movie page and threw it to the floor in disgust. He began perspiring again for the first time since his jog. His breath wheezed audibly and he squinched his eyes, trying to eradicate from memory the movie page he had just explored. Rick was no prude, no skipping Pollyanna in a pastel bonnet; he lived in the real world, but he had hoped to find something on the movie page worth seeing — perhaps the life story of some whiskered scientist who conquered some dreaded disease after a ascetical lifetime locked away in his laboratory, or perhaps a boy on a ranch with his first pony — just some simple victory of some person over something terribly challenging.

He had searched for something worth going into town to see, something not necessarily sugary sweet, but at least triumphant somehow, in the spirit of man's struggle with himself or his world. However, the movie page was only a bombed-out city.

Rick sulked. He didn't want to turn the television on again, and his door bell still had not rung, so he turned to other sections of the newspaper. In the first section he traced the hapless plight of some Soviet seaman, smacked about as a limp shuttlecock in a badminton game by the major powers as they postured and jockeyed for political advantage with his little human story, their creation of center-stage drama. The specter of nuclear war was about us all, and the two major powers in their infinite wisdom were diverting attention to a confused sailor.

Rick read about a balanced budget for his country by the year 1991, when another pack of "movers and shakers" would be in office to deal then with this problem, a hot potato now politely dropped by a forum of erudite potentates unwilling to squarely face the truth themselves. Rick knew the truth on this subject. When, he wondered, will somebody at the real helm have the guts to say what needs to be said?

He acted out a charade in his own family room, sliding an ottoman to the middle of the rug for service as his Hyde Park soapbox. He stood weavingly on it, before an invisible rostrum and microphone, nodding in all directions, acknowledging applause. Then he hushed the multitude with calming pleas from outstretched hands.

"Ladies and gentlemen," he began, after meticulously brushing his bedraggled jogging suit, as he had a half hour earlier, thinking two honest-to-goodness costumed kids were going to turn at his street, "I have an important announcement to make. It seems that our national debt simply cannot be paid, nor can we simply remove it and start from scratch again to save the house of cards over which it has mounted and proliferated. I, as your president, am completely lost for a solution to this thorniest of all problems facing us on the home front. If any of you out there listening and watching in television land have any suggestions on how we can save our system, kindly contact me personally at the White House. Seriously, I haven't the foggiest notion of what to do and all of us up here are at our wit's end. We thought no harm could come from throwing this problem open to our general public to see if someone, somewhere, might suggest a better way of solving it than we seem to be doing."

Rick stepped gingerly down from his family room ottoman and again slapped a damp thigh still sausaged in a pant leg. It wasn't a happy slap, just an unrejoicing, "in-your-face" slap of candor chased with a dose of frustration.

He sat down in his lounger with a final vocal salvo.

"The government would not quality for a Visa or Master-Card under the same guidelines that John Q. Public must follow. Utter lunacy."

Rick snatched through the remaining sections of the morning newspaper, darting from article to article, trying to sift truth from the dusty prairie of equine feces which seemed littered about on nearly every page. He read about the Halloween monitors checking for razorblades and poison in candy, trooping around in their vests of phosphorescent brillance with their whistles at the ready like stripped referees in a ball game. Whistles? They would have been the laughingstock of the entire Bronx two generations ago.

Cranking down the footrest of his lounger, sending it disappearing into the base of the rocker, Rick lumbered to his front door. He opened it cautiously, afraid to see an empty front yard. His supposition was correct. Nothing much had changed. The bright brain of his pumpkin was dull-witted now, stuttered with faint bloodflow of light and its mouth lolled stupidly.

He returned outside to his chair, but this time he sat edgily near the front, poised for possible sad retreat back into his house. He slung the creased remains of the newspaper into his lap and rummaged for the business page and the editorial page, two last bastions which offered from time to time some glimmer of hope, some ray of clear understanding in the war zone of doubletalk.

Often the business writers wrote truth, regardless of the repercussions it caused. Rick casually knew one of these writers, and he always felt good when this muckraker of establishment ennui and complacency stirred that cold pot a little with the unsettling ladle of concern.

The latest flap, championed by this writer, was a restatement of some congressional statement concerning the disuse of credit cards by the public in order to force a cut in their usurious interest rates; and thereby, through this drying boycott of spending habit, the public themselves could help return the country to fiscal responsibility.

Rick hoped the idea would germinate. He had cut up his own cards years ago. He chortled and slapped his thigh again.

Wouldn't it be great sending those money changers behind closed doors for a boardroom sweat-box session over sharply reduced Christmas shopping?

Rick could envision the stately water pitcher on those mahogany conference tables getting quite a workout. It would be as rich as the peasants marching out to Versailles and making Louis XIV put down his muttonchop and drumstick long enough to appear on the balcony.

In a rush of personal perspicuity, Rick decided to call his casual friend, the business writer at the newspaper, whom he thought was the business editor now, or at least *should* certainly be the business editor by now, considering his steady flow of marvelous work.

It was eight o'clock, two full hours after total darkness, but Rick hoped that perhaps he was still there, laboring over some juicy deadline with which to arch a few eyebrows the following morning. Rick was in rare form, aflame with the clear portent of the moment. He stood flatfooted, punching in the numbers on the kitchen wall phone, but he could have been standing atop his family room ottoman again.

The answering party at the correct department searched for the writer, but reported that he had left the building only minutes before. Rick was undaunted.

"Will you speak with me a minute?" inquired Rick urgently.

"Yes," came the wary response.

"I needed to call somebody," blurted Rick.

"That's fine."

"You know I'm out here in the suburbs on Halloween, and not one kid has been by my house."

"I see."

"Sad, that's what it is, sad. It's too sad even for tears. You know what this is, don't you? Don't you?"

Rick didn't wait for an answer. He charged ahead, his Hyde Park sermon delivered over the line with the gusto of a nineteenth century circuit preacher.

"I'll tell you what it is. It's a microcosm of a larger macrocosm — a microcosm of agony in a larger macrocosm of same."

Rick paused, fearful that his buttonholed listener wouldn't understand him and might even hang up.

"Yes," the newspaperman replied agreeably.

The way in which he replied, his inflection, his tone, demonstrated emphatically that he understood Rick's reference. He proceeded.

"That's exactly what it is. We may have a few more conveniences nowadays to lord our precious vanity over the animals, but really, societally, we're regressing.

"Yes," repeated the newspaperman laconically.

Rick charged further. He had not been derailed by impatience or disinterest on the other end, so he beat his drum again, relating his conversation with his dad earlier that evening about Halloween nights in the old Bronx.

"I can believe that," offered the newspaperman.

"The bad, bad Bronx, mind you," reaffirmed Rick.

"Yes," comforted the listener.

"Well, thanks for hearing me out. I had to call somebody. Tell everyone to keep writing those fidgeting bombshells of truth."

Rick asked to be remembered to his former acquaintance, the fine writer, the reason for his call. The polite shoulder upon which Rick has vented his fusillade of emotion promised that he would mention their conservation.

Placing the receiver slowly back on the hook and sighing wearily, he strode back through his house and once again flung himself down outside into his patio chair. The stub of candle in his pumpkin sputtered in doddering old age.

Rick sat for a long time, with a slump of resignation, sharply different from the stiff-backed anticipation which had occasioned earlier the near miss of those two children, who had approached within a block of his driveway. There would be no imitation goblins this year. It was too late for them now. In the stillness, Rick thought he heard the faint laughter of children three or four blocks away. He didn't even incline an ear, knowing that they wouldn't be coming his way.

In the blackness of his front porch, illuminated now only by the two orange bug lights, with his pumpkin shutting down its face for good, Rick restyled that which he had long harbored in his mind as truth — that which others with a line to sell had tried to dismiss offhandedly as silly negativism. He couldn't wriggle out from under the stern yoke this time. It pressed down with invisible force, resolutely locking its tawdry bondage upon him.

Despite what he was being told, or was being led to believe subtly by screen, sign, or page, the state of life for man was steadily worsening. Admittedly, man's showy conveniences, the baubles of his dark vanity, were refining with passing time, but his real progress with himself, socially, culturally was retreating and unmistakably so, regardless of what would masquerade as truth to the contrary.

Rick realized despicably that the only hope for man was vanity, not love. There had never been enough love and never would there be enough love. Love, which could save man so easily, would never be plentifully in season with its silos spilling munificent bounty. There might be enough vanity around for man, however, sifting out of bins, overflowing cisterns and tanks, streaming opulently through shielding containers to be trodden and mixed with his dust itself.

Maybe man was looking in the wrong places for his answers. Maybe in searching for enough love, his groping quest ought to turn up his own vanity, collective, ubiquitous, scorpioned under all rocks. Then, perhaps, man would see finally the true tenuity and fragility of his existence.

"I wish it were different!" cried Rick. "I'd give my life if it were different," he proclaimed.

Rick treadmilled inside his house again and returned to his patio chair with a creased and worn scrap of manuscript. He bent toward the dim light and unfolded the wrinkled paper, which he had rooted from its secret, resting place within his family room bookcase where he kept copies of his favorite pearls of wisdom, words penned by some of the great minds in literature.

Rick considered these sixty-four words on the battered page before him, words uttered by the immortal John Steinbeck's character Doc, in his 1945 novel *Cannery Row,* as the greatest paragraph he had ever read. He wanted to pour over the words once again this evening.

* * *

"It has always seemed strange to me," said Doc. "The things we admire in men, kindness and generosity, openness, honesty, understanding, and feeling, are the concomitants of failure in our system. And those traits we detest, sharpness, greed, acquisitiveness, meanness, egotism, and self-interest, are the traits of success. And while men admire the quality of the first, they love the produce of the second."

* * *

Rick pressed the yellowing page, folded now nearly to disintegration, in the safety of his trembling hand. A black housecat, with a diamond of white plunged between glowing eyes, highstepped stealthily in the dewy grass a few feet from Rick's dark outpost. The cat, a distant daughter of a sabre-toothed tiger, phantasmal tonight through the gloom of Halloween, meowed and bristled when she spotted Rick, and then she pranced away, watching Rick regardantly until she disappeared within the cape of blackness.

Rick rose stagily, creakily, and bent to blow out the puny flame. He folded from the waist, down into the cave of the pumpkin, removing its scalp by its stem. He blew where its brain would have been had it owned one, and politely, almost reverently, closed its eyes and mouth to dumbness with an euthanasic puff of air.

He negotiated the front door for the last time that evening. Blindly, he poked for the doorknob, which swam hazily before his liquid eyes. He trudged down his dimly lit hall to his bedroom.

A slittering cockroach scurried across the wall before him at the height of his sloping head. His eye, peripherally, caught its mad scramble to safety. Rick barked a knuckle on the wall, trying to swat it down, but the cockroach was too elusive. It dodged Rick's aerial assault and survived, reaching refuge. And so they had for a long time, long before man, and probably would long after man.

Rick wondered if they ever laughed at us. No, he supposed, cockroaches weren't intelligent enough to laugh — just intelligent enough to survive.

A GIANT STEP

The miles droned by hypnotically, the tires thumping measured clacks as they drummed across the seamed expanses of interstate highway.

A confused hurricane, maddeningly indecisive in the Gulf of Mexico, revolving in stalled fury one hundred and fifty miles beneath this ribbon of whisking road, had curtailed vehicular traffic flow. No great exodus of fleeing beach residents had yet begun, however, to clutter the road with baggage-laden conveyances of escape. Stan, his son, and his son's girlfriend had the concrete boulevard practically to themselves this late summer afternoon.

Stan lounged across the backseat, pillowed up and daydreaming, tingling with the vivid memory of the morning scarcely passed. It had gone well, better than he had expected. He grew drowsy in the humming car and bathed his eyes in darkness, replete with the happy promise of future expectations.

What a consummate professional she had been. Almost all of her suggestions on copy editing had been solid pluses. She had ruled his manuscripts, sent ahead to her by mail two weeks before their five-hour motor trip to the state capital, with thoughtful, redline considerations, each brightening the thrust of his work without emasculating his individual style.

Their hammer-session with line-by-line editing had proceeded fluidly, with a bare minimum of literary disagreement. Her skill at smoothing his "basically clean copy" was adroitly melodic, persuasion blended with her genteel carriage as a woman of quality. Stan had acquiesced to nearly every copy correction, and the scant few they didn't alter together as they progressed, he had agreed to polish later at his home for return to her through the mail.

When they had conferred on money matters, with her son, the president of the publishing house, at the conclusion of their proofing session, Stan had asked the two "heart balm" questions he had vowed the day before on their long drive to have courage enough to ask.

As Stan's son continued behind the steering wheel, Stan closed his eyes and relived the last, edgy minutes of their morning meeting — those moments when he had received the two answers he desperately had to hear. His son and his girlfriend spoke breathlessly in the front seat, sensing Stan's exultation of spirit, and respecting his chosen quietude.

"Tell me honestly," he had begun, "truly honestly, apart from any lousy fee you can make on this first book of mine, do I or do I not, here at mid-life, have enough raw talent to trot out something worthwhile or should I run along like a nice fellow and store these dreams on some dusty shelf?"

The reply had been instantaneous, unwavering, without time allotted for a conjured falsehood. Any polygraph test at that moment would have scored sincerity for the utterer.

"The talent is there, unquestioned. It can't be taught, only improved. Yes, you're good enough — excellent in fact. I would tell you differently if I thought so," she replied with assurance.

Stan had let air escape thankfully through his lips. He had smiled relievably, while fumbling with the knotted necktie at his throat. Stan often fumbled with his tie, boosting himself mentally when things weren't going well, and other times too, when he looked good and felt secure and confident. *Now for the clincher* thought Stan.

Stan scooted forward in his chair, the way a band student is instructed to edge forward just before the opening fall of the baton, to best create diaphragmatic participation in the music.

Awaiting Stan's second question, the elegant, late middle-aged editor perched ambassadorily in her chair, with a gracile air etched along her slender countenance. Her son, an author too as well as an executive, sat quietly behind his working desk, letting his mother do most of the talking. He had not read Stan's manuscripts.

"Given the talent, which you so graciously say is there, what are my chances of buttonholing some publishing house in New York, and selling this book over the transom as they say, on the spot?"

She laughed decorously.

"I mean I could make the rounds to all the waiting rooms of publishing houses with say a neon bowtie on, that flashed off and on."

She laughed again, a trifle more unchecked with her mirth.

"Knowing my hunger, my zeal, my selling ability, I could camp out in New York. Maybe with letters of introduction sent ahead, some executive would bite in the vein of 'we'll pay you and take our chances; short stories are back.'"

She answered with the sharp, kind firmness of a Mother Superior chastising a young nun over the grievous nature of her "not-so-sinful" first violation of rules behind the new walls.

"Regrettably, even with your excellent talent, one chance in a million."

The pause was interminable, seemingly a fossil epoch in duration, though only a few moments actually passed.

"I thought you would say that," Stan slumped. "Well," he replied slowly, plunging a nervous hand against his knotted throat again, "we go. Mail me a contract and I'll get you off a check from home. I had to hear your answers to both questions first."

Stan took a short turn at the wheel, spelling his son midway on their five-hour trip home. He captained their voyage from the comparative loneliness of the west-to-east interstate highway, which laced across the brow of the state, with a right-angled turn onto the far busier north-to-south artery of commerce and tourism. There, despite the petulant lurk of hurricane, the three travelers noticed an immediate intensity of truck traffic. It would take some hurricane indeed to prevent the brawling, blunt-brained trucks from delivering perishable goods from Atlanta distribution points to the lucrative, pantry dollar of the South Florida markets.

Drizzling rain had started again, dripping from a pewter sky, relentlessly, morbidly, without thunder or lightning accompaniment. It was the kind of fine droplet weeping which gloomily taxes only the intermittent sweep button on the wiper control, the variety which foretells of a hurricane about, somewhere close, catching its breath offshore before it selects its situs of final tongue lashing upon the land.

Painfully Stan reviewed the events of the past week. The steady rain, impassive shover of enemy soldiers marching now through his mind, thrust him back to the problem at home. The brief respite at the beginning of their return trip, that interlude orchestrated by teasing strips of light canvas sky,

allowing him to sun himself in the radiance of his meeting
with his editor, was no longer there. It was rudely removed
now by the dome of gray everywhere above him.

As they motored closer to home, the misery was focusing
again. Late summer rains, drowning the center part of the state,
had pelted for days along a squall line, reminiscent of the
normal summer deluges he had recalled as a boy growing up
in Central Florida. These sheeting rains, slaking water table
thirst, had been conspicuously absent for several years. Old
timers, however, had steadfastly ruminated about their eventual return. True to cracker prophecy, they had returned to
Central Florida this late August, unannounced after an unex-
plained absence of nearly a decade.

* * *

The plumbing had backed up through his home, wetting the
carpet with odoriferous messages of stain. A new septic tank
was needed and a new drain field would have to be coffined
throughout his front year. Stan hated the thought of the expense, just at this pivotal point in his life when he needed to
help finance the launching of his satellite writing career with
the publishing of his first book.

His home needed a completely new roof and he already had
a leaky patio roof that was getting progressively worse. He
had started to pack cotton in his ears when he was home alone
during rainstorms so he could watch his sport and nature
programming without the auditory reminder of the leaky patio
roof. The mocking sound of the gushing leak outside, only
a few feet beyond the sliding glass door behind his family room
rocker, distressed him dreadfully. During rainstorms, when his
family was home, he avoided what would result as needed

explanation for cotton earplugs by moving to the sofa, a few more blessed feet from the splatter on the patio floor. Stan fought to remain in a positive frame of mind. The morning meeting had been such a success. His writing, two years of early morning diligence, scratched out at his dining room table while his family slept, had been his salvation amid the persistent, horrible nightmare of his treadmilling business career.

By most standards, he made a good living — not marvelous by any means, but a good and solid income. His career had gone absolutely nowhere for five years, however. His income range had clutched as a bleak, browning bush to a wind-raked plateau, while he had fought those five years to maintain his base of clientele.

Excessive rate structuring, comparative shopping among his mobile and price-conscious clients chasing jobs in the Sunbelt and stringent underwriting guidelines for new and existing business had produced a skyrocketing attrition rate of twenty percent a year in his policy count within his insurance agency. In the early years of his career, the attrition rate from "move-aways," malcontents with company claims service, company price-jumpers, and those who left because they disapproved of the left side part in Stan's hair, had been a manageable six to eight percent a year.

The attrition rate for existing business was now galloping away uncontrollably. Only periodic rate increases had maintained his income on its stationary plateau. He couldn't replace twenty percent of his policy count each year. No other insurance agent with their company in his metropolitan area had been able to experience any real policy growth either.

Stan had survived for now, balancing his agency precariously over a quicksand bog of unpopular rate increases while scrambling madly to replace a portion each year of the twenty percent escape of accounts which passed unceremoniously out the rear door of his agency without saying goodbye. It wasn't pleasant, that trudge and stumble path to the office each day.

Stan drove on, barely at the speed limit, mesmerized by the monotonous slapping of the wiper blade. The excitement of the morning meeting and the agony of his experiences at home and at work emoted alternatively in his brain. To his left, great trucks thundered by, spraying the station wagon with cartwheels of oily rainwater. Their husky, rectangular power shook the car with miniature earthquakes as they churned past with delivery times in distant markets hustling them judiciously beyond the speed limit, within patrolling trooper allowances for breaking the law.

During his five-year struggle to stay afloat, his expenses, with a growing family, had accelerated. Normal inflation, extra vehicles at home, new college costs — all had come along to gobble the line-wedged pie chart of his paycheck. It wasn't the fault of his family. It was just the way things happen. He had never dreamed he would be this miserable in mid-life, remaining in a state of dazed plodding most of the time.

Stan stated his case at home repeatedly. They understood, he supposed. It was difficult for those who loved him and knew his fine mind to fathom his newly wrought mediocrity in wresting a family fortune for them. They didn't speak up against him, but he discerned a masqueraded look in their faces. He ought to be more successful, they fashioned privately without rancor, oblivious to their telltale expressions of muted confusion.

He chased every opportunity to demonstrate his normalcy

and to illustrate that he was not just copping out with a bad, misguided attitude. When fellow agents in the metropolitan area failed, chucking in the proverbial towel, he would painfully report to his lovely family that he had remained afloat, albeit adrift, clinging to business wreckage throughout, sustained by a managerial division of policies from the sinking agencies, to those who survived.

Within this glum scenario, with Stan seeking understanding, while trudging month after month to his office, the insidious plot had thickened. He realized horribly that he could no longer hold any other corporate job within the ensnaring morass of industry. His wife became increasingly exasperated with him. She pleaded with him to do something else — to get going again.

He couldn't. He was trapped. Now so raw and feverish with anti-establishmentitus, he could never get a second wind again in any new corporate whirlpool. It has passed him by, and he knew it.

He was so consumed with doubt, worry, and loss of faith that he could never again fake the falseness required to be a corporate success. His health was beginning to erode and his teeth needed attention. Thank God he had gotten his drinking under control. His writing, his blessed escape valve, dictated that he just couldn't drink too much and write well. Miraculously, he had realized that.

Vulturine business burnout had taken up perpetual lodging in his body like snowbird visitors arriving in the Sunbelt for a fatiguing stay with distant relatives. Stan knew he would be destroyed ultimately by business, as the central character in Hemingway's *The Old Man and the Sea* was destroyed by his environment. And, he would probably lose the respect of his family. They never would understand why he was so able, so qualified, yet so seemingly stifled. They knew not the warden of business imprisonment who cruelly locked out the freedom of his real talents.

Perhaps his vindication would come later in his life, if he survived, so their passing misunderstanding didn't plague him. He didn't dwell on it. They might understand later that it had taken more courage to step off the establishment carousel than to remain on that spinning turntable that never really led anywhere. He would never relish their apology in the hollow smugness of "I told you so," if it were ever to be offered to him, later, clear-sightedly with the passage of time. Stan had very little pride or vanity any more, and a pound of flesh only meant something good to eat for an empty belly, not "one-upmanship" in stroking one senseless ego at the expense of another.

Destroyed, yet, but never defeated! Hemingway was right.

There was, however, one scintilla of hope for Stan — one needle-pricked aperture of hope, through which pink and violet stealth of dawn could filter.

He could write like the wind, in howling gales, if need be, and in whispering zephyrs, too, when it was decorous to speak in a light, breezy mood. The words streamed out in torrents of feeling. He wrote desperately, commitably, completely, as a man with only one remaining chance to live. Fury led his hand, fury to write well, to experience and live something worthwhile — fury above the dusty, bottomless, vine-chocked abyss of his business life.

As he wrote, it became easier and he came to understand himself more. His dashed confidence, dross from the crucible of business, was collecting itself again, piece by piece.

* * *

Passengered with Stan, his son, and his son's girlfriend, the drooling rain hitchhiked along without invitation, the entire way on their returning motor trip, right into Stan's driveway at home. One of the longest weeks in Stan's life wickedly awaited his return.

Smelly water was extracted from carpets, and his front yard was carved up like an archaeological dig. Dinosaur machines broke his driveway with plod-heavy, grunting stumbles of work, running down their footbelt, then waddling over it with stertorous indelicacy. All this was being done so his bathroom would work again. His indoor outhouse was flushing away his grubstake allowance for the financing of his first book of short stories.

Would he ever be able to do something worthwhile? Would he ever be able to test the literary waters with his work, to see if he could belong, or would he be ever destined to only dream of his first book, imprisoned forever in the gooey quagmire of a derailed business career, forever paying for unexpected emergencies like burrowing drain fields in his front yard?

Would his manuscripts only be found in the wreckage of his death, when his personal effects were sorted out? Would they be discovered by some concerned party sorting out his stacks of ledger pads after his early passing? Would they be discovered only then, when some priceless soul interrupted the sorting of his shirts for charity and his books for the library, to sit on the edge of the bed where he died of a broken heart, to read hour after hour in the thrall of his work? Would he ever get anywhere with his work or would septic tanks at home and similar monetary diversions at his lonely office sentence him to a moiling, lifetime encapsulation in utter obscurity? His mind flighted to psychedelic flashes of fright. He saw himself voiceless, puny, Lilliputian, banging unseen on the inside of a suspended bubble displayed invisibly on the banquet table of literary publishers. The publishers, who gorged themselves on the literary sweetmeats of other authors, remaining blind to his pounded bubble.

Somehow Stan survived the week. The plumber overcharged him and didn't do the work properly. The electrician's bill was a shock in electric blue. The septic tank people damaged more driveway than they said they would damage. The rain pelted down incessantly.

During the endless week, his editor telephoned, checking on the sending of the first check for the proofing and the typesetting, the price they had both agreed upon the previous week. Delicately, Stan put her off for a few days, with a whistle, whip, and chair, using a persuasive speech that all was fine, a ruse that some monies had to be transferred from one financial institution to another, his explanation for the transfer of money from his shallow pocket to shallow, cold pipe in the ground.

There is a sadness beyond tears, a sadness of defeat that one accepts without malice or coldness, only numbness. No rancor. No bitterness. Beyond those portals is its acceptance. Just chisel strokes with lopped chips that fall away unnoticed at your feet to blend with the lost earth, destroying a once lovely statute to faceless rubble, is that catatonic sadness, quiet as stone itself.

* * *

The last visiting fixer saviour to the carnage of Stan's front year was the concrete man. Stan had counted his dollars all week as the threadbare orphan boy counts his meager coinage arriving by school bus at his first carnival. Still, through it all, he clung to the hope that he could make a contract payment on his first book. He looked terrible but he hadn't drunk a drop of liquor all week. He had been afraid to drink. He had wanted to get bombed but he knew he couldn't cope if he had.

The concrete man arrived in his dilapidated pickup trick, which was badly in need of a paint job it would never receive. His work apparently was so abrasively dusty that it had always proved more prudent to junk the trucks before finally having to paint them. He chugged to a gasping stop, down the circular driveway where it began to curve by Stan's home, just at the spot where a dirty gash of earth remained — where underground drainfield pipe had tunneled under broken and removed concrete.

Stan shuffled out to meet him, hearing the sputtering truck approach when it was still a block away. The driver creaked from the cab of the truck wearing crusted rubber boots. Before offering a work-chipped paw to Stan, he slapped his hands to his thighs, against stiff, concrete-laden khaki pants, sending a cloud of granulated dust billowing about the two of them. Stan closed his eyes protectively against the dust. Closing his eyes had been reflex action all week, involving anything to do with money for that blasted septic tank, so he had no difficulty shutting his eyes.

The concrete man was stringy and tough, a fiesty rusty wire of a man who looked as though he could be bent but not broken. Nut-brown from work in the sun, his strap-lean arms showed every pipe in their circulatory system. The left breast pocket of his salty workshirt tumored in a bulge from his leathered chest. Within this pocket was enough paraphernalia to fill a dowager's purse. Dog-eared scraps of scrawled work estimates; a caved pack of Camel cigarettes; a gleaming Zippo lighter, a picket fence of rubber-ended pencils, and a doddering loose-leaf pad bandaged by Scotch tape and strategically placed paper clips made his bony chest on the left side appear like one-half of an inflated life preserver.

When he began to walk about the circular driveway, assessing the needed repairs, Stan dogged his steps with supplied assurances that not everyone who lived out here in fashionable suburbia was rich. The grizzled old gent said little. He appeared not to hear Stan's disclaimer. He continued walking, pacing off the broken concrete with paces of a full yard that made him look like a German soldier on parade. Stan managed to toss in his line about his wife working and leaving for work before seven o'clock each morning. With that truthful but soap operatic appeal for a fair estimate, the old gent donated a weak smile of understanding.

Stan showed him the removed section of concrete in the circular driveway through which the sumppump drainline had been laid, then described the other three driveway panels which had been busted by the cracking onslaught of the marauding machine. Of course the old gent easily saw everything, ignoring Stan's windy dictum that was being trotted out with as much gesticulating verve as a college fund-raiser stumping a rich alumnus.

Stan obliged the reticent gent in meekly holding one end of his tape measure as he gauged distances all about the damaged area. The silence was deafening. The concrete man circumnavigated the driveway again, alone, then propped himself across a tired fender of his truck and began to unload the accoutrements of the ciphering moment from his left shirt pocket. Stan stood by glumly as a roped prisoner-of-war, expecting the worst.

Deliberately the old gent laid his quiver of pencils in a row next to his soiled pad and selected a yellow stub of graphite as a surgeon asks for an opening scalpel. He wet the tip on his tongue and, after laboring through a wheezing draw on a bent Camel cigarette, huddled over his figures. Stan feared that mathematics were not his long suit, but allowed somehow that concrete estimates with homespun arithmetic might indeed be within his power to create, for someone like himself who really would prefer not to hear any of it.

"Wire mesh," he murmured, and he scratched away on his pad.

"Wire mesh?" quizzed Stan. He received no answer.

"Break it up," continued the concrete man, mouthing each step after licking the tip of his pencil again.

Stan thought he understood. He nodded confidently to no one.

"Truck it out," he continued.

Stan nodded again fearfully, realizing each step in the estimate meant more money — money that had been squirreled passionately aside for his first book.

"Frames," listed the old gent.

Stan pulsated Martian green. He was still sick over the wire mesh. A huge, invisible dollar sign hung down from Stan's concerned forehead.

"Eighteen yards to bring in," he ciphered audibly, repeating each step innocently, unaware of Stan's agony.

Stan paced around in little circles away from the truck and poked at clods of hard earth, recently routed from damp sleep by the great machine.

"Finish and level," croaked the old gent with an unintended telegram of finality in his voice.

Stan sighed, his chest sagging unceremoniously. The old gent burrowed deep down into his lined pad, agonizing over the figures. The numbers slurred in his brain, only from lack of formal schooling, not from lack of natural intelligence. Stan looked up wistfully at the trees. In the light breeze, they appeared to sob in bending omniscience, seeming to understand as erudite elders.

The concrete executioner pawed over another cigarette, ringing the white paper with a dusty clamp of forefinger. Unlike Stan, he had never been schooled in proper closing techniques in sales. He pinched the jugular vein with announcement of his hieroglyphic estimate, but did so without malice or conjured design.

"Eight hundred and twenty-five dollars."

"Eight hundred and twenty-five dollars!" squealed Stan. His eyes rolled skyward.

"Yup. She figures eight hundred and twenty-five dollars," he replied, rechecking his addition, squinting down the lined page.

"You realize we're talking three concrete panels, not an interstate highway from Nome to Key West.

The old gent shrugged.

"You got break out, sledge hammer stuff. Old wire mesh don't break out easy ever' time. You got truck out. Even if I bring another truck with a hydraulic tailgate, it ain't easy. You got . . ."

He listed all the steps in the process but Stan didn't hear him. He slumped against the truck, muttering.

The old gent folded his little pad carefully.

"Whole lot of money just to go round and round, ain't it?, he yawned dryly.

Stan swiveled his head slowly in the direction of the concrete man, returning from the paralytic state of shock which had robbed his consciousness when the estimate had first been read.

"What was that?" he demanded. "Repeat what you just said." He sprung erect from the slumping lean of support provided by the dusty truck.

"I said a whole lot of money just to go round and round." He shrugged, oblivious to the sagacious poignancy of his remark.

"Round and round," whispered Stan. He formed the words slowly and savored them as fine Cognac after a splendid meal. His eyes widened and his heart skipped. "Yes, that's it. Round and round. Yes. Yes."

Stan grasped the old gent and shook him with the vigor of a displaced person seeing a loved one again. Concrete dust billowed again in the air.

"Yes!" he shouted. "You've done it. Thanks."

The sun-raisined concrete seer weaved under Stan's shoulder embrace and dropped his latest Camel from his open mouth.

"I got the job then?" he asked, staring whitely up at Stan. All his blood has been rocked down to his rubber boots.

"Yes ... I mean ... no," blurted Stan. He tunneled down into his pants pocket and scrounged a folded five dollar bill. "Here, for the estimate, your time."

Stan ground the bill into his calloused paw and escorted him by the elbow from the fender of his truck to its driver-side door. He practically lifted him up to his tuft-torn, vinyl seat.

"We don't do no job right now?" he queried to Stan, happy to be clinging to his steering wheel again and no longer shook as sagebrush in a sandstorm.

"Thanks, but no. but really yes. You wouldn't understand. I can't tell you how glad I am that you came by today."

The old gent backed slowly out of the broken driveway, still an easy exit, although the level construction scar didn't lend itself to the beautification of Stan's premises. The concrete man wagged his head with incredulity. Nice enough guy spoke his puzzled eyes, but never would he understand these suburban jokers, corkscrewed his brown face. His little pickup truck clanked away in battered first gear.

The white postal jeep, trimmed in blue and red, entered Stan's cul-de-sac on its daily run and passed the bucking pickup as it left the quiet street. Stan had five minutes before it would hedgehop around to his mailbox. Bathed in white hope, communed in spirit, he dashed inside his house and scribbled off the first check to his editor. In his haste, he cut his lip on the sharp paper when he sealed the envelope with saliva. He thumbed a stamp crookedly on the envelope and raced outside again.

Perhaps God looks after those who bite off more than they can chew, and then they find some way to chew it, Stan pondered prayerfully.

He could hear the approaching postal jeep throbbing in neutral, just out of view behind shrubbery next door at his neighbor's mailbox. He loped up his driveway, stopped briefly at the ugly scar in the concrete, and then with a smile of victory, took a gallant, giant step across it. He slipped the envelope into the black box and rung up the red flag just as the postman slid to a stop. They waved to each other.

Stan's envelope was consigned to a city five hours away by auto, the state capital upstate at the other end of that horrible August rain. It had a second address however, one superimposed with invisible ink discernible only by Stan. Really, the envelope was sent to himself.

The rain was over. The sun was out. The unfeeling circular driveway with its jagged scar didn't look too bad in the sun. It would have to learn a little patience, that driveway. Its time would come. Stan knew all about patience. His time had come.

THE PEDAL
FROM THE METAL

Pumping furiously, his knees pistons of churning fury, the sun-bronzed teenager turned his skeletal bike onto the sidewalk at the end of his sloping driveway and began to pace the nudging, bumper-riding stream of late afternoon traffic which had spilled down from the nearby expressway ramp.

The edging boulevard on which the cars had bunched was only tantalizingly close, by at least another thirty minutes, to eventual stoppages for weary businessmen in their suburban garages. Until they collapsed at home, they would be punished by angry, creeping traffic, a final, harrowing anthem to their frantic day in the city.

The teenager sported a yellow ballcap, worn catcher-style with its bill cocked up at the rear, a sleeveless T-shirt which exposed his "pumped-iron" biceps, and a jagged pair of denim cutaways, scissored unevenly above his knees. Sockless, his summer tan blended uniformly where socks would have hidden sun, down past his ankles to the curve of his sneakered shoetops.

His bike was stripped for speed. It boasted no elaborate system of gears and chains for creating speed on its own. It was simply a bike, devoid of chrome at every adorning place for chrome to be. The handle bars, sloped low like floppy dog ears, appeared too large for the skimpy frame. The rear tire was the original black one, but the front tire was a white-walled, patched antique, giving the bike an altered air of snooty urbanity which failed miserably, given its other collections of middle-class plainness.

Outfitted for day riding only with no hint of headlight or red reflector, generous strips of phosphorescent night tape clued any observer that perhaps, just perhaps, that bike occasionally slipped out after dark, prowling sidewalks and ducking police cars, in order to trade a rock tape, claim a special baseball card, or pick up a homework assignment prepared by a neighborhood girlfriend.

Along the snake of honking traffic, grousing at the crawl of his captured plight, Mr. Collins had noticed the bike, peripherally, when it had first zoomed out of its driveway to begin pacing the beetling creep of homebound cars. For over a mile, on its ribbon of sidewalk, the bike and its urging master paced Mr. Collin's car, sometimes remaining in full sight a half-block ahead of his purr-idle luxury sedan, and occasionally falling somewhat behind when a sudden green light allowed a dozen autos to proceed hurriedly before the persistent amber light slowed traffic again.

On two occasions, when he caught a slow-advance sign at a construction site, and again, when a policeman waved him past a harmless accident, Mr. Collins thought he had swatted the bike from view, as one repels a buzzing, pesky gnat from a twitching nose. However, well into the second mile in this undeclared race of bike and car, the sleek kid reappeared, having caught up again, first standing on the pedals pumping frantically for thrust, and then squatting back on the seat with his powerful legs split at a forty-five degree angle to rest them from oxygen depletion while manufactured speed allowed a short, coasting respite.

"Damn it," scowled Mr. Collins, clenching his steering wheel. "Where the hell is that kid going?"

Ahead, somewhere in the late afternoon glare of shimmering metal, a stalled car smoked with its sprung hood diagnosing evident heat stroke. The crocodile of cars beeped and nudged. Harried businessmen, silk ties flapping in the breeze, yelled out their windows and then in abject defeat, awaiting a policeman to wave them around the sick vehicle, dropped their coated white sleeves defeatedly out their windows.

Unlike the spring-wound businessmen, workers riding in pickup trucks simply popped extra beers from hidden caches and placed them in little, brown bags for ostrich-like drinking, joking and laughing the delay away. They seemed to handle the inevitable setbacks to smooth motoring progress better than the businessmen.

"Damn it," repeated Mr. Collins, "where the devil is he going? He's passed a half-dozen convenience stores. He can't be out fetching milk or bread for his mother."

Mr. Collins knew for certain where he was going — at least for that afternoon. His ultimate destination, for his life, was debatable, as he never took time to analyze what he really was about. He was too busy haranguing his sales force week after week with the urgency of business machine sales quotas.

This late Friday, he was headed for his health spa. He churned privately. If his secretary hadn't shook a pretty fist of unanswered phone calls in his face at 4:30 P.M., he would have beaten this traffic snarl. He would have been halfway through the gauntlet of pain on the clacking chrome machines, and only minutes away from the blessed sag of suet in the steam room. Now, here he was, ensnared in a sticky Venus flytrap of traffic, having plowed through those phone messages as fast as possible in maintaining some semblance of managerial professionalism.

He daydreamed, stopped in line, edging ahead in line. Exhaust fumes from pausing, trembling vehicles invaded the domain of natural air and rudely offended the nasal passageways to his brain. He twitched his nose annoyingly and carded his forehead with a deep palm-press of one hand. A workout at the spa was mandatory this late afternoon to prepare his middle-aged body for an onslaught of rich food and drink later that evening.

He and his wife were dining at the club with their younger friends, the Jamiesons. He supposed he would have to match Tim Jamieson, nine years his junior, drink for foaming drink, in order to peacock his virility to his own wife, then make the best of laboring through two hours of bridge afterward at the Jamieson's home. That insipid Friday night card-playing knell had tolled eight straight losses at the bridge table, and eight consecutive quiet rides home, unspoken punishment for suspected poor play, which was really quite passable by most governing standards.

Into the third mile of their unproclaimed sprint, Mr. Collins pulled ahead by several blocks, when traffic exiting at two large shopping centers slowed the kid to a walking, sidewalk portage of his bike through the labyrinthine exodus of bag-stacked station wagons funneling onto the broad boulevard. Baring his teeth gleefully, Mr. Collins saw the kid grow smaller in his rearview mirror, logjammed at the shopping center within the murky river of vehicles.

Then, shamefully, he erased his wolfish sneer, experiencing a freshet of ice-cold, prickled alarm across the surface of his skin, realizing he was competing as he would at his office —

competing with some kid he didn't even know, over really nothing. Was this the horrible residue of years in the workplace?

Mr. Collins was annoyed. He didn't like that competitive monster stampeding loose within him. The slowing traffic ahead bestowed a mulling moment, allowing him to examine the real truth about the situation. He couldn't escape the disquieting honesty that emerged.

Beginning the fourth mile since encountering the bike-piloting kid, and the last mile, thankfully, before the spa shrine would finally be reached, the kid pulled even again when Mr. Collins was the last car to be halted by the blinking, clanking semaphores at the one railroad crossing on the route. He cursed unthinkingly, seething within his earless caisson of metal. Then, he trailed off placidly, almost feebly, relaxing desperately, recalling his stern self-examination of himself a few minutes earlier.

The late arriving train had not shown around the bend, yet the sensored semaphores restrained the cars. The black-on-white bars bounced lightly, having attained their horizontal positioning. The kid appeared beside Mr. Collins' stymied car, and simply walked his bike around the horizontal tentacles of warning. He bumped over the double line of track, then hopped aboard again with legs split for coasting balance. He sped off, his legs pistoning furiously again.

"Hey!" shouted Mr. Collins aloud, "is that legal? Why should he be allowed to . . .?" Again, he had succumbed to the straitjacketing maiden of his business world. He caught himself. Shuddering, he pawed his five o'clock stubble, trying to relax, torturously awaiting the train which was now approaching as a gathering dot far down the tracks.

"Wonder where that kid's going? Emergency, errand, or what?"

The orange caboose clacked past. A gray-capped old man with a sooty face waved down from the little pillbox to frantically waving bundles of young children, who were bounding about shriekingly in the halted station wagon idling abreast of Mr. Collins in the adjoining lane of traffic.

"Clear sailing now," Mr. Collins sighed. For the last sprint to the health spa, billboard-genic at the next intersection, he revved his engine all the way up to a yawning 40 miles per hour. This last dash was always the easiest, as subdivisional cocoons with alluring names siphoned off weary commuters on either side of the boulevard, thinning congestion for those still tread-milled to the concrete conveyor.

He zoomed into the health spa parking lot and shoehorned his long, shiny car into a tiny space designed for a compact car. He slumped momentarily in his seat, and trailed a long gasp of weariness into the air, weariness with his work week and with his four-mile gauntlet run from the interstate ramp and his self-proclaimed, after-hours duel with the kid on the bike. He hadn't seen the bike since the pokey train had obscured it from view five minutes earlier.

Mr. Collins puffed out the driverside door of his car, suffocating his duffel bag of fresh, workout togs in his right hand, as he similarly choked his brown briefcase all day long in that same hand when he made his business calls. He weaved through a turmoil of cars and stepped stiffly up onto the sidewalk, directly before the portals of pain themselves, the imposing glass doors of the spa.

There, pressed against the entrance, with a cupped hand as helpful visor against the tinted opaqueness of glass, and his perspiring nose flattened with pugilistic deformity below his sweat-leaking hand, stood the kid from the bike race. "You beat me here, didn't you?" snapped Mr. Collins, without true rancor in his voice. He sat his duffel bag on the concrete sidewalk, held his wandering belly tautly, and with his free hands now on his hips, surveyed the neck-swiveling kid.

"Pardon me," answered the kid politely, stepping back from the glass doors. Confusion furrowed his forehead.

"You beat me here," shrugged Mr. Collins. "Don't I look familiar?"

"No, I don't understand," stammered the kid, vertically inspecting Mr. Collins from head to toe for telltale badges, chevrons, insignia, or any other sign of authoritative officialdom.

Mr. Collins smiled and softened his interrogation.

"I saw you come out your driveway four miles back, thirty minutes ago. We paced each other all the way here. That is, young man, until you slipped past those railroad signals. Remember?"

"Yes and no," parceled out the kid diplomatically, about as free with information as a teenage gang member asked to rat on a buddy.

"I mean, I rode over from my house, but you, I mean, so many cars and me on the bike, watchin' out on sidewalks and all. I . . ."

Mr. Collins raised his hand, palmed it skyward revealing no weaponry, and wagged his head with a smile.

"Stop! Whoa! Sorry, I assumed you saw me. Naturally, you didn't. You were on the bike concentrating. I was one of many cars. Let me back up."

The kid relaxed too. His ropy muscles slackened and he smiled genuinely for the first time. He tugged at his cap, removed it from his wet mop of straw hair, creased the bill, then replaced it on his head.

Mr. Collins bent his knees and gathered up the straps of his duffel bag.

"You going in? You a member here?" beckoned Mr. Collins to the health spa entrance.

"No," answered the kid, "like to though, I guess. We can't afford nothing like this — my family I mean. I work out on my own. I just ride down here 'bout once a week to look at the fancy stuff through the glass."

Mr. Collins surveyed the kid from head to toe, the way the kid had inspected him moments earlier. There wasn't an ounce of fat on him. He could have carried the torch into the stadium at any Olympiad.

"You don't need this place," observed Mr. Collins. "Save your money. You could whip your weight in wildcats, it looks to me. This place is $90.00 a month. It's overrated, really. It's getting as congested as that road back there."

He jerked his neck toward the four-mile stretch of carbon monoxided boulevard behind them.

"Yeah, it's pretty bad out there," agreed the kid, sweeping his eyes toward the boulevard. "But I can usually sprint back home this time of evening. Traffic eases up pretty soon now. I usually pump it pretty hard all the way back and then hit fifty push-ups as soon as I get off my bike."

"Fifty?" stated Mr. Collins dryly, fighting an expression of envy.

"Sometimes seventy-five." The kid smiled, wanting to please.

"Save your money," finalized Mr. Collins. "You're doing it the natural way." He whisked behind the glass doors, trailing a fatherly goodbye over his shoulder.

The castle of pain inside sparkled with an array of dazzling chrome monstrosities which resembled faceless, skeletal dinosaurs. Their bones clattered as alive, when stacked discs of weight, an arm or plodding leg of metal, clanked from one place to another.

Throughout the workout area, wall mirrors were everywhere, reflecting narcissistic satisfaction for the tribute to sweat and grunt. Soft light, psychological hues of pink, tangerine, and cool blue — light engineered to create the right mental atmosphere in redistributing triglycerides and hidden pools of uric acid, bounced into every remote corner of the metal reformatory.

Protoplasm jiggled everywhere. Real aficionadoes in the warfare against advancing age sported the proper equipage for battle — solid color shorts, designer T-shirts, white socks with neat rings of color at the top, washer-scrubbed sneakers, and color-coordinated wrist sweatlets and headbands. However, the uniformed *and* ununiformed "argyle set" gaspingly dropped puny dumbbells, puffing around in boxer shorts with horrid black dress socks stretched up on chalky, pudgy legs.

Delighted in being far removed from that pursy conglomeration of accrued fat, jocularly known as the "argyle set," as he was in better than average condition for a man his age, Mr. Collins closed his eyes to their wheezing, bumbling attempts at exercise, and ran a hand again over his five o'clock advance of darkening shadow.

Better get to it, he sorted resignedly. Some semblance of defense was needed for the Jamieson drinking bout and a highly probable ninth straight, inglorious defeat at the bridge table. He popped a chalky antacid tablet in his mouth from a trusty vial hidden deep in his coat pocket, belched decorously, and began to ungarrote his neck, dragging his satin tie from under his slippery, fine-clothed collar.

When Mr. Collins paddled past the front desk on the way to his locker, Murray, the white-smocked desk attendant saluted him.

"Oh, Mr. Collins?"

Murray, the front desk guru, who always hared it rapidly throughout the spa, doubled as laundry clerk, tripled as substitute masseur at critical busy times, and quadrupled as assistant business manager for the henchmen concealed behind their cubed cells on the second floor.

"What's up Murray?" cautioned Mr. Collins suspiciously.

"Promotions."

"Promotions?" Mr. Collins asked, glancing about him, thinking himself still ensnared by the lasso of his downtown office.

"Promotions, from the top," urged Murray, waving a rolled towel hand in the direction of the second floor.

"Listen, I know you're well off Mr. Collins, so don't take this as pressure or anything, but I wanted you to know. I was instructed to tell everybody."

"Make it snappy, will you Murray? I got a date with the Spanish Inquisition."

"Okay. Any guest resulting in a membership, exclusive use of the eucalyptus-scented sleeping room, no charge for one month, and a free massage. Two guests, resulting in membership, free locker fee for six months and no towel fee either for six months. Three memberships, ditto, right, memberships resulting, one full month free on any membership renewal, plus, get this, twenty percent credit back on your initiation fee . . . that fee that seems to be so unpopular with everyone."

Murray grinned sheepishly, wishing he hadn't voiced that hushed remark concerning the exorbitant initiation fee that management was down-playing.

"Murray," spat Mr. Collins, sloped flaggingly against the counter at the chest-high reception desk, "we don't need a lot of new members. The steam room looks like a bazaar on market day now."

"Oh, come on now," defended Murray hollowly.

"Yes, exactly that. You got to wait in line at peak times to sweat off the lard, plus the Black Hole of Calcutta steam room, once you finally get in, sounds like an international economic summit. Everybody is jawing everyone else on their own importance — a double suffer. People are in there wishing they had a limp business card to pass over to you while you drip."

"Aw! Mr. Collins, c'mon," cracked Murray weakly.

"C'mon nothing. We don't need a big promo on new members. It's expensive enough now to provide the right tax shelters for those dudes hiding out on the second floor."

"I don't make the rules. They want me to tell everybody when they come in. Anyhow, the promotions are good for the rest of the fiscal year, until September 30th," concluded Murray, putting a stack of folded towels on the top of the counter, knowing he had done his job, regardless of its credit or worth.

"Fiscal year? Give me a break! Am I in a health spa or a vault at the Federal Reserve?" mumbled Mr. Collins.

"I didn't hear you; say again please," inclined Murray.

Mr. Collins mutely waved a hand as answer and trudged off for his long-awaited half-hour appointment with Dante's earth-bound, suburban Inferno.

In the exercise room, upbeat polonaises of wide-awake music rushed everyone puppet-like through their exercise routines.

Mr. Collins slung some dumbbells around, then mounted a diabolical dinosaur, saddling aboard like some character in a Spielberg creation.

Minutes later, wrung and wound as a slopping dishrag, he extricated himself from the clutch of the gargantuan praying mantis and noodle-legged past the sleeping morgue on his way to the steam room. The machine seemed to sneer fiendishly after him, voraciously waiting for its next hapless rider.

The sleeping room door was ajar. He glanced in to find several sheeted, near cadavers snoring in Friday evening collapse. One corpulent executive, tabled on his back, stretched out like an entire range of lumpy mountains. Just then the cracking staccato of the intercommunications systems barked a request for Murray to come to the second floor. Two oppressed businessmen, slumbering on slabs of cushioned table, jerked at the strident blast, as if they had been given electric shock treatments. Mr. Collins walked past, shaking his head and clicking his teeth. Poor devils, they were asleep, probably trying to forget their own Tim Jamieson.

The roller coaster gyrations of the stock market was the topic under discussion outside the weeping glass door of the steam room. A line had formed to worship Hades. Mr. Collins shuffled his bare feet and hung his head, choosing not to lend his personal view on the future course for market investments to the melee of opinions already formidably presented.

Finally his wait was rewarded with a narrow spot opening for him on the top bench inside the misting cell. He withdrew totally for a few minutes, counting dully the droplets of perspiration plunking from his chin. Only the pestering thought of the evening before him nagged his consciousness.

All the towels in the great rubber drum outside the steam

room apparently were in use elsewhere when Mr. Collins paroled himself from his self-slavery. After his shower, jerry-built with a translucent wafer of soap he scrounged up from the shower drain, he settled for drying off with an extra T-shirt he had stowed in his locker. There was no attendant anywhere near the locker room. Mr. Collins assumed they were hawking membership promotions near the outside entrance. He dressed, leaving the knot of his tie loose at his throat. A glisten of perspiration, heat-baked from his workout and steambath, broke the surface of his body and dampened his shirt at his spine. Grabbing his unopened duffel bag, he wandered out of the locker room toward the entrance. He wondered why he had tugged along the bag in the first place. He didn't need aftershave fragrance or deodorant for his empty auto. There would be plenty of time to suit up, after a cooler shower at home, when he regrettably trussed up a couple of hours later for the 8:30 p.m. pilgrimage to the club and their date with the Jamiesons.

"Oh, Mr. Collins, got just a minute?" begged Murray from his reception desk, having returned to towel folding duties after withering at attention before a barky audience in the executives' offices on the second floor. "Only a minute, please."

Mr. Collins reluctantly sauntered near the command post, wanting instead to make a beeline for the front door. Murray clung to his desk like an unsmiling, robed judge remaining safe and high on his somber perch. He didn't come down to mix lightly with Mr. Collins as he had done while showcasing the promotions a half-hour earlier.

"Listen, I didn't mention it when you came in. Well, those three businessmen you sent by last week, from out of town, who came for just a steam?"

"Yes, what about them?"

"Well, I've got to charge you the new guest fee on them, $10.00 each, I'm afraid."

"Aw, c'mon, Murray, what cooks?" Mr. Collins scowled. His duffel bag made another fast trip to the floor.

"New rules."

"Those guys weren't here twenty minutes. They said so. A lousy steam to soak out a slug of Bloody Marys flying in on the 'redeye' from L.A., and it's $10.00 a throw? I haven't had a guest here for months."

"New rules from above, not me." Murray again smoothed a stack of neatly arranged towels, a stack much more useful somewhere else, perhaps in the empty plastic drum outside the steam room.

"And the reason for the new rules, Murray?" Mr. Collins asked coldly, folding his arms across his coated chest. Mr. Collins knew that the second floor, corporate office walls had one-way mirrors in certain, secreted places. Now he realized the reason for Murray's important summons there when he had walked by the sleeping room.

"Well, they say with the congestion in here, more and more all the time, they got be more strict on guests."

"Ah," blurted Mr. Collins, stabbing an index finger wildly into the air while tripping over his duffel bag. Every pair of eyes within thirty feet rotated instantly in Mr. Collins' direction. "Got'cha this time, Murray."

Murray wrinkled his nose and patted his stack of towels for security.

"Murray, when I came in here a half-hour ago, you were booming me on promos for new memberships. Increase the membership was your lecture, right? Now you say the congestion in here has produced a stricter guest policy."

Murray nervously fumbled with the towels. He pulsated crimson and grinned sheepishly. There was no cross-examination of witnesses. Mr. Collins' case was ready for the jury.

"Stick that $30.00 for those three guests on my current bill, and, Murray, when the bookkeeper sends it, make that bill my final one."

Mr. Collins collected his duffel bag and paced jauntily toward the glass doors.

"Mr. Collins, Mr. Collins!" Murray called after him. Originality in correctly stating his name was all the rhetoric Murray could muster.

* * *

Mr. Collins' bike was a little more elaborate than the kid's bike, but still a darn fine workout machine, without pulleys and gears doing all the work. A fancier bike was allowable for Mr. Collins. After all, although he was in pretty good physical condition for middle age, he wasn't seventeen!

He had carted it home preciously in the trunk of his car the night before. It had stood patiently in his garage overnight, gleaming at the ready, at attention on its kickstand, coiled expectantly for its Friday night first spin through the streets of his neighborhood.

Mr. Collins was supremely happy. He had won a battle, one seemingly small and insignificant, but nevertheless a great battle indeed. He had come within a smidgeon of buying an odometer for his handlebars at the bike shop. He had thought it important to keep track of his pedaled miles on his new, portable spa, but, at the last moment he had relented, recalling his scolding of himself over his frightful competition with the kid on the busy boulevard the week before. The odometer would have been the same as Monday morning sales quotas. When he got tired, he would just quit riding, he decided.

His old baseball cap from college, smacked clean of layered dust from a long Rip Van Winkle repose in his hall closet was perched snugly, catcher-style, atop Mr. Collins' head as he chugged up his driveway on Friday evening.

He did, just a mite, resemble that grinning kid with his own ancient, cardboard-billed ballcap turned backwards in the same fashion. The bridge defeats at the Jamiesons' had ended at eight. They were dusty antiquity now, as were remembrances of the ritzy spa.

Mr. Collins was becoming a mighty fine bike rider himself, and more importantly, he hadn't the remotest idea how many miles he had already pedaled.

THE HANDKERCHIEFS

Harry hated Christmas, complaining moodily that Christmas trees offered for sale at civic club lots cost as much as bicycles for kids used to cost, not to mention how the trees were now grown, dispassionately, in endless rows on huge farms, hastened to rapid maturity hundreds of miles away in other states.

Harry detested street and store decorations strung up closer and closer to Halloween, retreating boldly back through sacred Thanksgiving, headlong back without the barest apology, allowing commercializing business pursuits to steal an edge for sales with the display of early tinsel, trespassing and trampling all over that late November pause for thankful reflection.

He hated the dark-suited floor walkers in the gaudy department stores, sporting white carnations in their lapels and Cheshire cat grins across moist lips when cash registers clacked out their version of Christmas spirit. He loathed the pointed elbows from the megapodal tramp of dazzled shoppers, poking through crowds, rudely pushing as they jostled along, with bulging packages of intended merriment steamrolling a path before them.

Harry couldn't stand skidrow Santas, bleary-eyed at their posts, hawking passing motorists in front of shopping centers with poorly attached beards slung across scratchy faces and phony pillows sticking out comically about their skinny middles.

And, he winced each year when the long fire engine blared the arrival of Santa on Christmas Eve in his neighborhood. The clashing, grating blast of the fire engine whistle could be heard a mile away. The firemen laid on the whistle lever each year for at least an hour as they whisked Santa, clutching precariously on the hook-and-ladder, through a labyrinth of neighborhood streets, while quiet folk were just lighting candles and having a thoughtful reflection at early dusk on Christmas Eve.

Harry dreaded the thought of December 26, faces long and sullen, wearily glum on that great Christmas exchange day, when the same floor walkers in stores ho-hummed each other in the presence of the upcoming assault — the nose-pressed hoard breathing on the glass doors at ten a.m. with a myriad of wrong sizes and colors, stitch flaws and faults, and soiled merchandise to complain about.

* * *

Harry was no Scrooge, however. Any Tiny Tim, once old enough to reason and understand, would not have found him cold or cruel. Any Bob Crachett would have found him to be a generous and decent employer!

* * *

At Christmas, Harry didn't hate processions of white-robed children, singing down middle aisles of churches, or wandering choirs in hay wagons and flat bed trucks, spreading a medley of carols for appreciative shut-ins. He didn't loathe the smell of candy and fudge bubbling on kitchen stoves. He enjoyed the positioning of ornaments and old, family heirloom bric-a-brac about the house, folksy Christmas remembrances handed down through generations. And, he especially liked creating new ornaments for decoration from pine cones, holly, and sticky sprigs.

He could creep along without complaint within a queue of poky motorists to admire a live nativity scene presented at a church by some industrious youth group. He could clap people on their backs and offer them an eggnog when they chanced by his home over the holidays. He could buy cookies offered for sale at his front door. He could keep the pot boiling with coinage when he heard the tinkle of the little bell.

Christmas music, a stack of long-playing records on his stereo, was fine at that time of year, and he reveled in formal, family Christmas dinners and brisk, invigorating walks in the countryside before them, looking for mistletoe to hunger up the body for the turkey feast.

Harry could sit in a darkened family room, brightened only by the multi-colored twinkling of the Christmas tree, silently enraptured with Luciano Pavarotti singing Ave Maria on a network Christmas special. Quite opposite the slump of spirit with sullen and dreary shoppers fighting the crowds on anticlimactic December 26th, Harry had no problem with that date because he stayed out of the stores at peak times. Rather, the day after Christmas ushered in for him a fantastic, gastronomic week of sliced turkey sandwiches, garnished with icy lettuce and generous smears of cold mayonnaise, and beyond that, turkey carcass delicacies like hot turkey pie, and that last hurrah for the gallant bird, thick turkey soup.

* * *

What Harry really hated about Christmas was the garish commercialism and the hammering avalanche of the buying season, the consumptive store dictators babbling sweetly over public address systems — "buy, buy, buy!" "X" marked the sore spot with Harry. The "X" in Xmas, not Christmas spelled correctly.

Every year at Harry's home, along about Halloween, when the first tempting nip of changing climate teased the night air in the torrid south, the clarion call would go out — an announcement far and wide that it was time to gear up for Christmas. These trumpeters three — Harry's wife, his daughter, and his son — were good people and fairly wise shoppers, but they never failed to marshal their enthusiasm for a gift-laden Christmas, regardless of need or the availability of money.

Harry would start his yearly protest about Halloween in an effort to meekly hold up the inevitable bottom line of Christmas spending. He would cite expenses incurred for his son away at college, list evidence that American business was in a down cycle and that this event would influence him directly — and soon. He would conjure up all manner of excuse, real and imagined, to shame everyone into a prudent and parsimonious Christmas buying season.

He would find some way to hint that indeed his daughter's need for closet space had already spilled over into her brother's closet. He never mentioned to his wife that she had five times the clothes hangers in her closet, as he had in his own. He left well enough alone on that subject, as Harry and his wife disagreed on practically every major point in their lives anyhow, so there was no object in chasing a subject that was beyond persuasion or solution. She didn't buy unwisely and she wasn't a spendthrift — she just enjoyed Christmas. It was the giving she enjoyed, the materialistic giving. Harry chose other gifts, invisible ones he cherished, but he undoubtedly wrapped them poorly, as often as not.

Each year, as Autumn lengthened toward December, his family would pester him about what they could buy him for the big day. They would begin casually, off-handedly just after Halloween, then build their head of steam with more pointed questioning leading up to Thanksgiving. By early December, they were pleading with him to name something he desired, or at least something he could use.

They seated themselves before him, on the little ottoman at the foot of his family room rocker.

"Dad, we love you. You W-I-L-L be getting presents. We A-R-E buying for you again this year."

Harry would fight his battle every year, saying he didn't need a thing. He would list all of the things he already had, and present his case for no new presents as earnestly and convincingly as possible. In a light vein, he would often banter with them, hopeful they would become annoyed with him and drop the entire topic.

"Give me a cold, windy day of winter in a bottle that I can release on a day of my choice in August."

"Give me a permanent sabbatical from the ringing of the telephone."

"Give me a lifetime library card."

"Give me clean water, fires in the fireplace, and the ability to pay my bills."

"Give me a stolen moment with Diogenes along his quest on an open road. I would love to meet him."

"Dad, stop. You're being silly. It isn't the same, all of us opening presents and you with practically none. You're G-O-I-N-G to have presents." Their chorus was note perfect at the Met.

Harry knew each year that he would be defeated. They never really took him seriously. He worried about that. Harry lost his annual battles ultimately, when the remaining shopping day count slipped below ten. Battles he lost, but perhaps not the war. His protestations over the years had produced one, singular victory — Christmas for several years had been an endurance of green cash expenditures only, without implementation of any insidious plastic credit card assistance.

He would finally surrender with an appeasement of either socks, underwear, or handkerchiefs. Either of the three, inexpensive gifts would obviate opening the January and February mailbox with one peeking eye, with the rest of his timid countenance shying away from any possible stuffed cluster of bills. In very late December, during the last few, hectic shopping days, Harry would be cornered in his rocker, beat about the head and ears with loving, caring blows of cooing prattle from all three family members.

"Handkerchiefs," he capitulated. "Let it be handkerchiefs," he repeated wearily, waving a limp hand.

His family sighed happily. They had bettered him again.

Who was he, that quirky, strange, mysterious dad and husband of theirs, telling those who loved him that he didn't need anything?

"You just don't realize. We'll help you help yourself," they triumphantly decreed unilaterally.

"Handkerchiefs," Harry rasped in a whisper. "That will do fine."

The yearly summit conference was adjourned. Harry was vanquished, wilted in a defeat of love.

* * *

It was true that Harry's supply of handkerchiefs was somewhat limited and bedraggled. He owned five. Two, washing machine distressed, were as thin as tissue paper. Two others were frayed at the edges and rent with tiny rips. The fifth, Harry's favorite, had a large, practically indelible mustard stain once smeared on it at a summer picnic that was quite begrudgingly fading in color after each agitated tussle in the washer. However, these five, spunky cloths, rotated judiciously, blew Harry's nose and wiped Harry's brow satisfactorily.

Christmas morning arrived with as much anticipatory excitement for his family as in any past year. Harry had fussed to such a degree the last few shopping days that he felt tolerably good about the monetary outlay for commercializing the blessed day. Admittedly, more money had been spent than necessary, but at least nothing had been rung up on a ghastly plastic chit.

Everyone gathered in the family room for the opening of presents. Harry sat in his trusty blue robe that was quite serviceable again this year, although his wife had moaned all year that the robe really had to be replaced. Tissue paper, gift wrappings, and star-burst bows proliferated in rising mounds on the family room floor. There were several nice gifts for Harry's children, and several suitable ones for Harry's wife. Harry even had a couple of little boxes to open. Someone had wrapped an economy bottle of aftershave cologne for him, and he was also awarded three new pair of underwear to float in among his current dresser drawer contingent of holey and unelasticized derelicts.

Throughout the unwrapping session, Harry waded knee-deep to the kitchen periodically to refill his coffee mug, and each time in high-stepping gingerly back to his rocker with steaming Java, he began to realize, as the base of the tree became increasingly scanty with presents, that he hadn't seen his handkerchiefs.

Harry remained silent on the matter and stroked his stubbled, early morning chin thoughtfully. Thirty minutes later, the last package was split open and its indispensable booty unearthed for viewing. Still, amid the destruction of giftwrap on the family room floor, no sign was there anywhere of Harry's handkerchiefs. The base of the tree was now totally bare except for the white bedsheet, bearded in browning needles, draped about the tripoding stand.

Harry bit his tongue. No one mentioned the handkerchiefs. The cleanup of the family room floor began. The Board of Trade was now closed. Harry, bravely, had endured it. Now, the day really began for him — eggnog and brunch, not too much because the turkey would be served at 3:30 p.m., a heavy jacket for a brisk walk in the countryside, and visions of sugarplum fairies at noon, dancing in the form of NBA leaping basketballers, when the Christmas Day professional basketball game popped on the blinking Cyclops, well before the call to the dinner table.

There was no mention of Harry's missing handkerchiefs whatsoever.

* * *

Christmas was over and a normal routine returned to Harry's home. The new year pillowed down and the months skipped along lazily. The calendar shed layers of skin into spring, and then shied half-heartedly into the colliding breath of summer. Harry's old handkerchiefs, without fresh, new troop replacements, held up rather well even in the face of Harry's horrid, late winter cold. "Ole Mustard," their leader, lost a little more prominence of stain to the scrub of detergent, and the other four, already wafer thin and flappy with lengthening rips, struggled along courageously with their nose and brow duties. Late summer fizzled finally, and the brief Florida autumn arrived deliciously on a platter of splendid evenings. It was time again for the family to unveil their exuberance for gift-oriented Christmas, and time for Harry to post all his verbal rebuttals on college costs, utility costs, gasoline costs, and grocery costs in order to keep another Christmas bridled within the cobwebbed confines of his checkbook.

Two weeks before Christmas, Harry answered a plea from his wife to rummage through the garage storage area in order to transport back into the house all of the saved little boxes and leftover gift wrap from the previous year so that the new supply of Christmas largesse could be fussed up again with fancy packaging.

Harry stumbled and grumbled in the close confines of the storage area, lit dimly by the corded electrician's lamp, hung precariously by its hook and caged in its metal shield. As he had been instructed, he moved boxes, rolls of giftwrap, and handfuls of tidy bows up the stairs back into the house, muttering with every clomping step.

One little box, rousted from the darkness, felt just a mite heavier than the others. Harry examined it closely, holding it aloft under the extension light as an Egyptologist inspects a new treasure. He blew the film of dust off the little box as his eyes focused upon it.

Peeking through the cellophane in a neat, flat box of brilliant red were three of the nicest, folded handkerchiefs a nose or a brow could ever hope to see. Harry howled. He leaned back against the air-conditioning unit and howled again, one of those belly-tumbling laughs that makes one unexplainably sore the following day.

They were, of course, the handkerchiefs from the previous Christmas — Harry's weary acquiescence to his loving family's bombardment, purchased but overlooked last year in the whirlwind of wrapping. They had been transported inadvertently out to the storage area, hidden in bundles of unused boxes and wrapping paper.

Harry tiptoed into the house and carefully wrapped the slender box in this year's Christmas wrap. Then he smuggled the gift into the privacy of his bedroom, and stored it secretly under his bed, to await the perfect moment the following week when the gathering mound of new presents under the tree would provide proper disguise for floating in this tardy present from the previous year.

Days later, Christmas morning went well again. Harry propped himself in his rocker in his perfectly good robe and weathered against the cyclone of gift unwrapping. He held his breath when it came time for him to open his handkerchiefs. He poker-faced the moment as deftly as a cardslick receiving not even a pair of lowly deuces in the last, crucial hand of the night.

His heart beat excitedly. He was on the verge of great inner clarity and vindicated peace with himself. He could sense the portent of the moment. He made a fuss when the handkerchiefs were raised from their long sleep, saying he could certainly use them. What a thespian he had been — he had pulled it off. He was nominated for an Oscar!

His wife and two children did not tumble. Harry was vindicated. Each of them assumed one of the others had gotten the handkerchiefs. None realized they were left over from the year before.

Usually fathers don't win many battles with those family members who smother with their brand of love, but here was one battle won for Harry — a hard fought, undisputable victory for him alone.

The three new handkerchiefs were tussled in the washer several times to remove their smell of newness, then they were introduced as plebes into Harry's dresser drawer to take up lodging with the five upper classmen.

The new handkerchiefs didn't swagger there. Lordly "Ole Mustard" was handkerchief-in-chief there, a dresser drawer general to all. The new handkerchiefs became green lieutenants, learning their duties and earning the respect of Harry's nose and brow, doing scant dirty work last, mopping up after the affection and loyalty continued with the familiar, trusty five.

Harry never had been one to wander far from known routine.

BY THE MERCY OF
THE COURT

"Hey you, you can't stand there, buddy. C'mon, move."

"Stand where?"

"There, below da walk around, in them boxes. Where you at."

"Hour and a half until game time, ball park's hardly filling up," Jack declared with palms of both hands displayed skyward, revealing no hidden weapons beyond verbal protest.

"C'mon, move will ya. Ain't got time to argue wit ya. We get rid of people standin' like you doin' in them boxseat aisles! You got a reserved seat?"

"Yes, I have a seat," assured Jack, fighting a suffuse of purple rage which had begun to boil up through his coat.

"Use it then. Move, I'm sayin'," barked the seat attendant, looking like a threadbare, little archduke from a jerkwater duchy in his gaudily embroidered uniform of ballpark officialdom.

"I've got the damn seat you showed me up there twenty rows and you've got somewhere in your pocket the five spot I gave you for dusting off that seat with your dirty rag."

The feisty rooster slitted his eyes, groped among the million-footed tramp of baseball fans he had ordered about all season from April to this arrival of late October, and did, reluctantly, seem to recall Jack as indeed the true source of a crisp

Abraham Lincoln bill thrusted his way fifteen minutes earlier. The attendant pouched air in his cheeks, wheezed musty air from his charred lungs, reddened as a pinched thumb out to his red beacon of nose, and trembled agonizingly over the possible choice of an ever so mild apology to Jack. The hammering tongs of the great city, however, beaten upon him as mallet to brass, had, over the years, precluded the chance of even apology's stepbrother, basic and polite civility, of finding its tortured way to his lips.

"You gotta move. Them boxseat aisles stay open." He beat the crisp night air wildly with his dustmop hand.

Jack scowled, shook his head, but crated further attempt at hopeless duologue. He glumly returned up the incline of steps from the sea of empty orange seats. Pausing at the concrete walk around, he exacted sixteen ounces of verbal flesh.

"Hey, buddy, can you loan me five until payday?"

The attendant guttered a stream of choice one-liners over his retreating left epaulet, and hustled off to seek new fortune with gloved hand as lance, in his quest for another five spot bounty from some other out-of-town yokel. The understanding word that had almost surfaced when Jack and his tip had been recalled, coffined down for another long nap. The city had lidded again an awakening stir of kindness.

Jack and his son were in the big town, the one with the lady in the harbor, for the World Series — for the first two games — thrilled with the good fortune of knowing, back home, the manager of the host team, a pleasant circumstance which had sprung two precious tickets their way. What an experience awaited them — priceless for Jack, a four-decade, devoted fan of baseball, seeing his first World Series.

His son, who had galloped off for a concession stand when

they had entered the stadium, thereby missing the lively, forensic debate with the seat attendant, had flown up from college on a flight without frills, and Jack, grumbling with a upended piggybank, had secured the cheapest flight he could from his Florida home so they could be together.

Jack always braced himself when he went to the great city. Everything, one could possibly enjoy was there on that eleven-mile island, chocked and wedged on that rocky sliver of land purchased from the Indians for $24.00 worth of trinkets. But the people — it was brutal, dehumanizing! They had hands for tips as big as catchers mitts and smart mouths to match that needed a Mother Superior gargle, inflicted with liquid Drano.

Jack always cinched his belt really tight in the great city, to gird his loins so his guts wouldn't fall out on some street, disemboweled by cutting rudeness. He often wished he could snap on a suit of meshed mail, those found weighting down knights of old in museums, just to weather the ordeal of being a conscipuous tourist.

Jack hurried to the enchanting museums at every opportunity when he came to the great city, earmuffing the sides of his head and shutting his eyes as best he could, dashing between the oases of museum, hopeful to stay alive long enough along the streets to view with fascination the wonders in the grand buildings.

It wasn't the squalor in the city, as the city everywhere wasn't squalid; it wasn't even the congestion of robotic people in the city, as everywhere the city wasn't congested. He never fashioned himself better than the city people. He wasn't aloof. It was simply the rudeness, the vitriol of rudeness — dished out for no reason — that disturbed Jack. The eternal fuse of rudeness took most of the fun out of coming.

* * *

Alongside the throbbing bus at the airport, which had been named for the little, fireplug mayor who had read the kids the comics over the radio during a newspaper strike in the 1930's, Jack scrunched down below the belly of the bus, disappearing totally into the marsupial pouch of storage area in order to huff and puff his suitcase aboard for the trip across the river to the skyscraper borough.

The bus driver stood nearby like a wooden Indian, while Jack pulled stevedorean duty with his suitcase. When his lug-and-tug ordeal was over, Jack noticed a long bamboo stick, resting to one side in the storage bin — a prod for suitcase sliding, barely noticeable to someone not schooled in its intended use. Naturally, the bus driver had chosen to remain silent while Jack had pawed around on hands and knees.

When Jack and his son paid their fare to the same sour-puss minutes later, as the gray-smocked tortoise of slack-jaw gloom wandered down the aisle, Jack was prompted to blurt out, "And how long, my good man, before we reach Ossining upstate and the front doors of our new home, Sing Sing prison?" But he bit his lip, however, and only wagged his head. He looked out the bus window at the dome of pewter sky, and prayed for humanity and for no rain for either game that weekend.

Jack and his son checked into a marginal hotel. It was shrouded in perpetual shade, obliterated by taller buildings craning flower-like for sunlight, south of the theater district, practically in the shadow of the tall spire that had reigned as the world's tallest for four decades.

It wasn't the city's fault that the cockroaches clattered like racehorses across the cracked linoleum floor which curled up in spots like unclipped toenails. We can't pin that one on the big, bad city. It was Jack's fault alone that he acorned his money, all year long, into alphabet accounts, IRA, HR-10, 401k, and chose thereby to stay in hotels where the cockroaches were saddled and ridden.

The counter in the lobby of the hotel was protected by a cage of bulletproof glass, as though a Nazi war criminal kidnapped from South America were in the dock, protected from onlookers while they sorted concocted legalese over his obvious sentence of death. Transactions were conducted through an impersonal, fist-sized, low window with a concave bottom. Loose change could be retrieved by only the fingers of a concert pianist. Room keys were demanded for storage on a hooked board, behind the cage, whenever any guest earned a pass from the garrison.

"We's never, never had no bad ladies in no rooms, that's for sure," boasted the swarthy desk clerk, in explaining the policy on keys. He proudly arched his eyebrows toward the twelve floors above him. "No prostitute ladies in our hotel, ever, ever," he ranted on. Then his olive face eased, and he grinned fiendishly, confusedly, as if he really espoused the notion that virtue was its own real punishment, and he wondered where the true seat of Jack's libido resided.

Jack looked at himself up and down, affronted, wondering if somehow his attire or countenance had telegraphed in any manner a suggestion that he might escort some evening, a gum-smacking, stilt-shoed lovely away from her hell over a gaseous street vent on the cold street up to another hell in his warm hotel room.

Jack and his son sardined their suitcases into the closet called an elevator, nodding as they entered to a pencil-thin maid in a blue seersucker dress, who was squealing an ancient vacuum cleaner on rickety wheels over the slick lobby carpet.

On the bus trip across the river to the hotel, Jack had timidly smoked out his son's reaction to the two of them trooping all over the great city, during hours they had away from the game, to visit five haunts frequented by the great American novelist, Thomas Wolfe, when he had made the city the home of his galvanic pen in the 1920's and 1930's.

Ahead of his years with compassion and understanding, Jack's son, enrolled in a Southern literature class that term in college, unswerving to the beckoning allure of rock cafes and young adult distraction in the city, enthusiastically agreed to tag along on a shoe leather tour to all five locations.

Jack had breathed a sigh of relief with his son's willingness to accompany him. A Wolfe fanatic, lonely visitor to the Asheville gravesite and homestead of his near diety, Jack, a writer of fiction himself, had not wanted to tramp all over the city alone. He brightened with the magical promise of the vagabond excursion before them, and tapped lightly the scrap of paper in his breast pocket that listed the five addresses:

CHELSEA HOTEL   23rd Street
THE LOFT AT   13 E. 8th Street
THE HOUSE AT   236 E. 11th Street
       and the two in Brooklyn
THE HOUSE AT   5 Montague Terrace
NEARBY AT   111 Columbia Heights

There was one more address tucked away, 333 W. 76th Street, the brownstone mansion where Wolfe's paramour, Aline, had lived with her stockbroker husband, the site of his famous chapter "The Party at Jacks" in his celebrated work *You Can't Go Home Again.* Jack hadn't the heart to tell his son about this sixth address, considering himself lucky indeed to have been alloted agreeable nods on the subject of the five locations he had listed originally.

Off they hiked, Jack refreshed with a shower, setting out on their concrete journey Marco Polo style. Their first destination was the arty Chelsea Hotel, not faraway Cathay. The Chelsea Hotel, quaint, pink and rose in the late afternoon sun, with a confident air of eccentric probity about her, had a list of all her famous tenants scrolled on a plaque near the entrance.

Jack strolled in like a present tenant and immediately spied the faint remnants of cherubins and seraphins sketched on the high ceilings that were mentioned in passing by Wolfe in some of his works. Exuberantly, Jack, on the trail of dusty memorabilia, chatted unilaterally with the desk clerk and with a frosty administrator at her ancient desk. He wasn't allowed upstairs to visit Wolfe's actual apartment where he had stacked voluminous manuscripts in his bulky, wooden case, but Jack's eyes were bathed sufficiently and he was well pleased.

Not one hundred yards off a honking Greenwich Village thoroughfare, at West 11th Street, the neighborhood murmured as a hidden, sylvan glen. Quiet, well-manicured, brick houses, three and four stories in height, shouldered each other along the shady lane. They were solidly built, and each entrance was heralded by a grand flight of stone stairs. Trees, planted in earthen squares, stood tiptoe to glimpse the sun which winked briefly each afternoon across the window of sky between the two cliffs of building at the end of the street.

From the middle of the cobbled lane, Jack's son squeezed

off pictures of a refurbished house, where Wolfe once had lived. Jack climbed the steps and peered inside through curtainless windows at vacant rooms, high-ceilinged and newly painted. Open stepladders, stood over gleaming, shellaced floors, like giant capital letters leading off the alphabet.

A plump lady passing on the sidewalk, tented in a conical overcoat, questioned their camera and curiosity. "Any trouble there?" she asked, shifting her grocery bag defensively in her arms.

"Oh, no, nothing like that," Jack reassured her. "Thomas Wolfe, the famous author, once stayed here. That's all."

"Oh!" eyebrowed the woman, not at all disappointed with celebrity status decreed upon her very own street.

Back out into the late afternoon tidal wave of busy sidewalk they trudged, with one more address to find that day before a subway ride back to their hotel and a luxurious date with elevated feet, vacationed from the burning concrete of exploration.

Jack had reasoned that the chance of all five addresses still being in existence, as they existed half a century earlier, was remote. He knew some would remain — certainly the Chelsea Hotel for instance — but feared that some would be gone or altered beyond recognition. He was correct.

The loft on 8th Street, Wolfe's first real place of his own had winced under the pummeling sway of demolition ball. In the same spot rose a large apartment complex, and at ground level, a grocery store now claimed 13 East 8th Street. Jack sponged a long look at the neighborhood and framed capriciously how it might have appeared in Wolfe's day.

Still, Jack was pleased. Two out of three was decent archaelogical sifting for one afternoon, and best of all his son had gone along willingly, supplying companionship. Jack was so pleased that on their way to the nearest subway cavern, he stepped cheerily off the sidewalk by the canined curb three different times when nearly run down by suited halfbacks, with briefcases for pigskins.

* * *

The next morning, bright and early, Jack and his son left their cell in the sky. Their own key even worked in the door. His son awakened bouncily, noncommittal to his father's plans for the day, knowing they would be at a World Series game that evening.

Jack, animate with the success of the previous afternoon, voiced a desire to walk across the ancient bridge from one borough to another, just as Thomas Wolfe had done on those brooding, late-night jaunts of his own, when scene and character masterpieces cavorting in his cranium, were sorting properly for the printed page while he walked.

His son acquiesced, garnishing Jack's exuberance as parsley to a dinner plate. Aboard the twisting graffitied serpent underground, Jack confusedly negotiated their exit at the wrong stop. He couldn't get anyone to tell him where to get off (that only happened in the great city when one minded one's own business), and he couldn't fathom the wall maps on the speeding express.

He remembered seeing Brooklyn Bridge flash by, white signs on sturdy pillars, twenty years before, while training on Wall Street, when this son of his was also in New York with him, snug and forming in his mother's womb. He recalled that some trains zoomed over into Brooklyn, and Jack wanted to walk over the bridge on the pedestrian walkway. Guessing they were on a Wall Street train, he grumpily led his son off at Canal Street.

A mistake. Quite a hike remained to reach the Brooklyn Bridge, they soon discovered, but their trek was livened by the teeming tumult of chattering Saturday. Tourists, family groups, and guided excursions in long, innocent lines, swiveled their heads wonderously as they flocked down Mott Street, and along Pell Street in Chinatown.

Asian-Americans, slickered in white, wearing roomy black boots slopping wet from their work, hosed off the sidewalks in front of their cubbyhole storefronts, sending freshets of fishy water cascaded over curbing, delighting the dance-stepping tourists, who squealed on cue with holiday spirit in avoidance of the puny floods. Buckets of eel and monocled fish, dead with Poe-like leer of icy eye, collected at doorways and hacked lengths of squid, octopus, and exotic delicacies from the deep, hung salted on macabre metal racks in the store windows.

Past tenement towers they voyaged, glimpsing in the distance the butterfly spires of the old bridge. The blot of buildings against the morning orange was stilled this Saturday morning. They looked as curious as the statues on Easter Island, enigmatic, spires of teeming ecosystems, showing no movement above their lawns of dust and sand. A menagerie of variegated children giggled softly on a jungle gym and swung lazily on swings with their crooked arms elbowed about the chains. They dragged their sneakered feet in the scooped pits of dust, concavely excavated below each path of pendulous flight.

As they walked and walked, Jack's feet became flat, griddled pancakes, smarting on the cold stone pavement. Of solid, medium stature, Jack was a trifle short-legged for his height. He had to struggle to keep up with his son, who was practically stilt-legged at a full inch over six feet. His son strode easily at a gallop, while Jack puffed alongside him at a trot. Slowing his son in the shadow of the bridge with an outstretched hand placed loosely across to his chest, Jack snorted to a halt across a broad avenue from it. It looked over a hundred years old, every year of it. With a hand cupped as visor against the advancing sun, Jack surveyed one of the huge cassions he had read about. A marvel in its day, the bridge now appeared extremely well traveled.

"What do you say we grab a cab?" allowed Jack, looking over painfully at his son after gloomily assessing his feet.

"Fine. Sure."

"I mean we can still cross as we intended, just trading a cab ride for a wooden walkway. It will almost be the same."

Jack always apologized profusely when he changed his mind about things.

"We'll get some breakfast in Brooklyn and have a go at those two other addresses for Wolfe."

Jack flagged a cab. It slid to a stop at the curb, facing west in the opposite direction from Brooklyn. They tumbled into the back seat, lubricated across the scotch-taped vinyl on a drift of dust. The plexiglass shield between the two seats read them their rights.

DRIVER DOESN'T MAKE CHANGE

Feeling like thugs in a police roundup, Jack braced for a possible ordeal by motorized torture.

"Sir," Jack began, quaking just a mite, "please take us across the Brooklyn Bridge. Drop us just on the other side."

"Brooklyn Bridge?" startled the driver.

"Yes, over please."

"Hell, there's the bridge."

"Yes, I know. Just across please."

"Ya got me on da wrong side of da sonofobitch. I gotta loop around."

Jack closed his eyes, fighting the heat wave which was percolating up his neck from inside his sport coat. His son ground his teeth.

"We just made our decision there at the curb. We didn't file a flight plan ahead of time, sir."

"Gotta turn all da way around."

"That's the beauty of a car. I mean, you can turn around. The meter is running I believe, sir."

"#?X!*." His breath was audible, regrettably!

Jack looked out his window at the river, with the defeat of a sodbuster losing his entire stake in a sandstorm, spiked to his eyes. They were nearly across the third-of-a-mile bridge before Jack could collect himself to look for the wooden walkway. He missed locating it as they were across the vehicular gauntlet.

"This will be fine, close to that coffee shop up ahead," managed Jack, about convinced that the ultimate future of all civilized humanity was hopeless.

The driver wheeled his cage of orange to a halt, as far from Jack's pointed destination as possible, and yet close enough not to be obvious with his shun, at the unwise expense of losing a tip. Jack and his son exited with alacrity, expecting a mind field to explode at their skidding feet.

Jack simmered over his steaming coffee at their booth, warming his hands prayerlike about the cup. His son didn't say much, knowing his father was about to deliver one of his patented soliloquies.

He did, in trumps!

"I've long suspected it. This trip only ratifies my suspicion."

Jack waited for his son to respond.

"What's that, Dad?," he responded, nibbling at the bait.

"They punish you. Simply stated, they punish you."

"How's that?" feebled his son.

"Give them an easy trip, say on an expressway, or to an airport away from rush hour, and they'll sit there up front, ignore you indifferently, and dream of the tip at the end. But if you give them a fare for near the tourist traps, or near those awful squares, or a little out of their way like turning back toward the bridge, whammo, they punish you." Jack pierced the air with a wagging index finger.

Jack's son never bought all of his father's theories on things, having a mind of his own fertile enough to form its own conclusions, but he agreed privately across his face that his father certainly had a very convincing argument on this subject of taxicab theatrics.

The breakfast was marvelous. Eggs smiled; toast, browned in lava-running butter, crunched perfectly; link sausages, as fat as fingers, twitched their noses. The food was always marvelous in the great city. The museums were marvelous always, the shows and plays too. Much to see in the great city was always marvelous. Only the people, the rude people, were determined, it always seemed, on ruining a perfectly good town.

Jack felt a mite better, licking the aftermath of breakfast from his glistening lips.

"What do we do now?" queried his son, noticing that his father's pin-pricked deflation of mood was lung-blown alive again, restored partially by the warming breakfast.

"We've come this far. Let's make some attempt at locating those two other addresses for Thomas Wolfe, and if we strike out, we'll grab a train back to the hotel, and hole up with a nap until time to go out to the game."

His son smiled broadly when he heard the possibility of a nap mentioned. It was always a five-star Lincoln and Douglas debate — who was the better Rip Van Winkle in their family, pillow-hound Jack or his sack whiz son.

As they were finishing up their breakfast, a well-dressed man with comfortable elegance entered the coffee shop and selected a counter stool, close to their booth. Harry had noticed him alight there as he was cooing softly over the last of his tangy sausage. He wore soft-soled shoes, perfect for any sidewalk ambler in the great city. Jack wished he had packed a similar pair for himself. Slacks, jacket, and V-neck sweater, richly woven, matching tones all, blended exquisitely together, down the totality of his medium height. A soft hat, warming his crown on this brisk morning in late October, hid most of his smoky hair, which was battleship gray but advancing steadily toward ultimate whiteness.

He sported an unoffensive stubble of Saturday whisker, not unkempt, just enough shadow to lend the notion that he shaved all week for something important, indulging himself often on a Saturday morning with a skipping of razor duty, only to dress up his face perhaps at midday, after a morning walk or errands dispensed about his neighborhood.

On a strange impulse, Jack rose from his booth, edged a few feet to the counter, and asked, "Excuse me, sir, may I ask you if by chance you have ever heard of a street here in Brooklyn called Montague Terrace?"

"Why, yes, I know where it is," he replied without hesitation.

"Wonderful!"

Jack smiled back at his son.

"By the way, you wouldn't know Columbia Heights? 111

Columbia Heights, to be exact?"

"Why yes, very close to Montague Terrace."

The stylish gent from his counter stool, began to diagram in the air the street maneuver necessary to reach the two addresses.

"You go up this block, as far as you can, turn left, and then . . ."

Jack listened intently, making the sides of a box in the air with one rigid hand, planting each turn in his mind.

"I think I can find them. Yes, good directions." Jack returned to his booth, thanking him profusely.

As chance had it, the stately gent, Jack, and his son congregated at the cash register at the same moment to pay their breakfast bill. They left together, gestering politely first passage to each other at the narrow doorway.

"Come on, I'm walking as I do, I'll take you up the block and point out the way."

Jack and his son whitened momentarily, realizing they were in the clutch of the great city. He seemed genuine enough, but one needed to be on guard at all times, in this brutish hold of a town where taxicabs were driven by Star Trek Klingons. After sideward glances of hesitation, Jack and his son fell into step abreast of the geography scholar from the coffee shop.

The day was glorious, clear and blue and breezy, the kind of day that tinctures all wounds of the spirit, gauzing and dabbing infections of travail with the tender pat of a mother doctoring a tricycle accident in the driveway of her own home. The air swelled in their lungs and roughhoused their exposed skin with cubby slap and bite, sending Jack's hot breakfast cooking through his arteries, perking song-and-dance merriment to his lengthening step.

Jack fully expected the refined gent to guide them a block or so in the right direction, so he could point out a distant turn well ahead that was crucial for them, and then continue on alone in another direction with his own morning walk. Instead, the city blocks tallied one, two, three, as they sauntered three abreast; their guide nearest the street, Jack in the middle, and his son to his right, trying his utmost to check his bounding stride in better sync with the strides of the elderly man, and his middleaged father.

The Musketeers, chatting more familiarly with every passing block, turned left and paraded in front of the famous Post Office. Jack recognized the building with its distinctive turret-like tower, recalling somewhere its enshrinement on some picture postcard he had seen.

"May I inquire of your work, sir?" explored Jack, now feeling more at ease with their cordial tour guide. His son felt comfortable too and was now immensely enjoying the running commentary between the two men.

"I'm a judge," he replied almost apologetically, without a barest hint of revered officialdom.

"Oh!" mused Jack, tautly lengthening his cheeks.

"I work there," he gestered up to his left as they passed the mammoth courthouse. He didn't inquire about Jack's line, but appeared raptly intent to hear about it when Jack began to develop his own state of all things, past and present.

"I'm in insurance and write fiction," stated Jack.

"Interesting."

"I mean, the two are not related. That is, not intended to be, but often are if you get my drift."

"Yes," nodded the gray hat. "I understand."

Jack laughed a little donkey bray at his cleverness.

"Insurance is my career but writing is what I love."

He glanced apprehensively to his right to note his son's reaction to his comment, a view often expressed to his son, which his son had come to understand and accept. His son knew he wasn't going off the deep end with his true love, writing, casting other responsibilities out the proverbial window with home and education to maintain for he and his younger sister.

Jack poked a little further.

"Been a judge long?"

"Why, yes, quite a while. I'm a Supreme Court justice now. I was in politics earlier, in the State House in Albany."

Jack tilted his head as a tough critic might do contemplating a smashing opening night at the theatre.

"I would guess, maybe Dewey, more Rockefeller era, certainly not Roosevelt."

"About right, Roosevelt would be a little early."

Every utterance from the kindly gent was wafted on a cushion of softly spoken tones. He lullabied the listener. Except for his spiffy dress, he could have passed for a Saturday morning feeder of pigeons so comfortably unassuming was he.

"I attended law school once," confessed Jack.

He nodded courteously, willing to hear more, only if Jack offered expansion of the topic.

"I knew the law but I wrote my exam answers like I now write my prose, sweeping and involved." Jack swung his arm for illustration and plunked it playfully against his son's iron abdomen, demonstrating how he flowered those law exam answers.

"Yes, that can happen," agreed the judge.

"Although I knew the law, I should have been more direct

and matter-of-fact with my answers. My prose answers made them suspicious. My wife and I courted each other in law school and we studied a lot together. She used to study far into the night at her place after we closed the library, terrified, because I knew so many facts. Yet, she made better grades than I did. Innocent really, but my involved answers went against me."

"Probably."

"Just as well, I'm a visionary, you know. Probably would have been a lousy attorney." Jack shrugged. The judge chuckled.

They walked up to a farmers' market strewn across the sidewalk near the courthouse, an array of wooded stalls as temporary as a gypsy encampment.

"They set up this way on the weekends, across the walkways but must change their position during the week when the crowds come out from the subways."

He beckoned to the empty mouth of a subway entrance, which gaped frozenly open this Saturday morning, as if gasping for breath from the press and shove of the work week now concluded.

"Montague Street," announced their guide with a gloved hand pointed west.

"So close," zested Jack.

"Your Montague Terrace is on up. I'll take you."

Jack and his son, now completely at ease agreed with a thank you, realizing the judge was having as much fun reliving his quite familiar strolls as they were, being entertained.

They walked up the gentle incline toward the river, having pointed out to them the fine restaurants for which the street was known. The scalloped awnings announcing their names, rippled in the October chill, slapping against their metal, skeletal supports, which clutched their flight from elopement with the urging wind. Jack wondered if all the representatives from the United Nations whisked across the river to take each meal at their very own international eatery, along this street of restaurants.

Before looking for Wolfe's 5 Montague Terrace, having the tributary of quiet terrace pointed out to them at the end of Montague Street, the band of three paused at the little monument that heralded the Battle of Long Island, fought there during the Revolutionary War.

Jack kept craning his neck back toward Montague Terrace, but remained calm and patient, as he could see ahead the wrought iron railing of the Promenade, so he reigned his galloping excitement, knowing he was in a cluster of Wolfe memorabilia at every turn.

"The Promenade, I recognize it from the cover of a Thomas Wolfe novel. The iron railing is depicted on the cover of his novel *You Can't Go Home Again*. Probably taken from this very spot," Jack philosophied.

The judge described the wharves across the river and tabulated the various needles in the sky. Jack and his son moaned wide-eyed at the tip of borough with its granite, steel, and glass obelisks in the clouds. They viewed close hand the gray, ghostly naval ships lapping at anchor.

"He used to pace along here at night, chain-smoking, brooding over character and scene development. I shiver," laughed Jack meekly.

The judge listed further points of interest across the river among the spires in the clouds. Then they strolled back to Montague Terrace, less than a hundred yards from the waterfront. Jack was in the lead, the bit chewing on his gum! Scaling the steps at 5 Montague Terrace, Jack peered into the vestibule, and rapped lightly. There was no answer. He proudly directed their attention up from below, as they waited on the sidewalk, to the plaque on the outside wall, which chronicled Wolfe's seclusion there a half century before, holed up with his companion genius moods and energy, as he sculpted one of his timeless works.

Jack inspected one of the tall, elegant windows, perhaps the very one through which Wolfe was looking, in one of the photographs of him, salvaged for posterity after his early, tragic death.

The adventurers padded over to Columbia Heights, against the wind which was steadily blowing through the low canyons between the elegant townhouses. The judge pointed out a renovated front of a building, which disguised, except to a sufficiently trained eye, the vestige of an old firestation from the days of horse-drawn fire apparatus. The wind slanted their walk, flattening their coats to their bodies and numbing their cheeks and chins with needled Novocain.

"Would you happen to have a tissue?" polled the judge, politely averting his running nose from Jack.

"No tissue, but here's my handkerchief."

"I can't use your only handkerchief," he protested.

"It's for noses that run. Please. I insist."

The judge reluctantly took the handkerchief and carefully channeled his embarrassment within the confines of the cloth. Then he folded Jack's handkerchief and kept it on alert duty, in the hand farthest from Jack and his son.

Jack bounded up the stone steps at 111 Columbia Heights and spread his cold nose against a sliver of window pane.

Inside the glass, lacy curtains curled delicately. He examined the high-ceilinged hallway, and judged it high enough for Wolfe's seventy-eight inch height. There was no activity inside, so Jack refrained from knocking as he had done exuberantly without thinking, only minutes earlier at 5 Montague Terrace.

Like a clanking radiator warming a country schoolhouse before the first bell of morning, the judge, toasty with schoolboy merriment, announced an annual festival ahead as they approached a shady side street. Laughter and music sped to them on a blast of north wind, well before they could actually see the happy gathering of people.

"The Cranberry Festival. Each year it is held. Very nice!"

Rickety card tables, draped with crocheted coverlets, and laden with bakery goodies, curbed in long lines along the tree-swept street. Aromas of ethnic delicacies blended in the cold air, offering enticement for every sniffing nose. The pleasant smell was universal in appeal, quite without zealous, nationalistic constraint. The wise air spun the recipes down the embassy of tables into a intoxicating mixture of nasal allure which defied segregational recapture.

Barbed wire, stout wall, machine gun turret and even petty prejudice unarmed, would have been powerless against the waft of air current which tantalized all twitching noses and hungry bellies, regardless of which vowel ended which surname at any of the tables.

Jack hoped that the judge's leaky nose wouldn't keep him from scenting the mysteries.

A music grinder tinned somewhere in the background. Loops of excited children snaked about, awaiting chaperoned rides atop toy-like saddles strapped to tiny Shetland ponies. The unhurried stroll through the quaint festival was melodic, devoid of barker harangue, graced with broad smiles and dancing eyes erupting across faces of variant shade and color. The agony of taxicab rides was as distant as dinosaurs at that moment, dimly exiled to an outpost of the mind, forgotten before the time of recorded history.

Jack clapped the judge warmly on his back as they walked when making an emphatic point. Friendship time warped ahead, lassoed in a few city blocks, as though the passing of each intersection chronicled a decade of experience between the judge and Jack.

At the unpretentious church where Henry Ward Beecher delivered his thunderous sermons during the American Civil War, the judge made every attempt to show them inside, but the wooden, white doors were locked, and they had to settle for a zoo-like stare through metal bars into the peaceful church courtyard. The modest church seemed so incongruous in its peaceful repose with the city standing up everywhere around it.

Jack wondered if the white doors, time scarred with marring bruises, had withstood mob clamor and even assembly by nighttime firetorch, when the great Abolitionist had rung eardrums from his fiery pulpit.

The judge doctored his nose again with Jack's handkerchief as they circled back near the courthouse.

"You keep that handkerchief," soothed Jack.

"I wouldn't give it back at all until I had it laundered," assured the judge.

"No, I mean for good. You keep it. It will be a link to this unforgettable Saturday morning we are having together."

"That's very nice. All right, I will keep it if you wish."

"Yes, that is what I'd like."

The three travelers returned to the shadow of the courthouse again, and shook hands all around. The judge didn't know about Jack's hostage flights in taxicabs or his innocent trouble with rude people in the great city but he received the distinct impression that his kindness had been so very special, because Jack said so emphatically.

"I hope someone else someday is as lucky as we were back in that coffee shop to have a Supreme Court Justice give them a two-hour tour of the real city here across the bridge."

"You are nice so say so. I enjoyed myself immensely."

Parting was swift, best that way, Jack felt. Descending down the steps of a subway cavern, he and his son saw the judge pad away, newspaper folded under one arm, smiling happily in the morning brightness. Jack wondered if the judge would befriend other tourists that Saturday morning as dutiful envoy of the city, as kind arbiter and pacifier for all unevidenced squabbles in yellow conveyances with rubber tires.

* * *

Bouyed upon an aircushion of inner warmth circulating through him because of his salvation Saturday, Jack floated down the elevator very early on Sunday morning. While his son still slept, he marched two blocks to a coffee shop, scarcely shivering.

He felt so good that he didn't even complain to himself about the cauldron of hot asphalt boiling in a wheeled vat outside the lobby of their hotel at Sunday daybreak. Nor did he frown skyward to the top of the twelve story building in an attempt to locate the terminus in the clouds for that linked pipe that had droned all weekend on the roof above their room, splattering down a layer of black sealant with its accompanying stench. Shucks, he had savored the fanciful aromas from the tables at the cranberry festival. It would take more than pungent, oily asphalt outside his window to break his new spirit for humanity.

A few, resolute prostitutes glumly remained on the street at dawn, scanty pickings from the night before forcing them to brave the raw morning still at their offices. They clutched their sequined purses under their shivering, painted faces and stamped their stepladdered feet over airvents in the streets, worshiping the warmth of escaping steam. When police cars stitched the city streets with woeful whine of siren, racing to crimes more heinous than their pitiful presence, they clopped back into the recesses of store fronts to hide among the mirrors and showcases.

A sheet of paper, in the coffee shop window, hawking a $2.99 breakfast special caught Jack's hungry eye. He entered and plopped on a squeaky stool, holding his elbows aloft while an attendant, smocked in white, swirled a dingy sponge across the flecked counter top.

"Up early," grinned the pot-bellied man.

Surely he was the owner, thought Jack. He puffed that definite air of ownership.

"Hungry," asserted Jack.

"Can fix."

He slid a mug of steaming coffee, not nearly full enough to spill, in front of Jack. The damp counter sailed it past Jack's stool almost a foot, like a misjudged putt running past the hole on a lightning fast golf green. The gauge of coffee urn jiggled slightly downward, like brown mercury in a giant thermometer.

"You from outa town, right?"

"Florida. Up for two Series games. We were able to get

tickets, no bigshot stuff."

Jack downplayed everything that had anything remotely to do with money, figuring he might not get fleeced as badly if he wore an insignia of "humble pie" on his sleeve. It usually helped. In this instance, he wanted that $2.99 breakfast special with no false impressions forming that he was an out-of-town slicker toting big bucks.

"Where in Florida?"

"Central."

"Hm'm. Anywhere near Winter Haven? Got an aunt in Winter Haven."

"Close by name only. Winter Springs, however."

"Hey, mebbe you may know her — Agnes Schweepner?"

"Oh! no," answered Jack quickly, waving both hands in self-defense. "There are four towns with the title Winter in them: Winter Park, Winter Garden, Winter Haven, and Winter Springs. Three are pretty close together but Winter Haven is sixty miles from me."

The owner appeared insulted that Jack didn't know Agnes Schweepner. He placed his red, meaty hands on his twin shelving of hip, after wiping his nose with a rolled sleeve wound up tightly at an elbow. His roped apron warred gaspingly against his heaving stomach.

"Got a buddy down there too, a buddy from Korea days. Lives in Saratoga. Ernie Trawick."

"No, not close. Don't you mean Sarasota, though? Saratoga's up here. Horses and all."

"Yeah, that's the place. Sarasota. Ernie Trawick in S-A-R-A-S-O-T-A."

Jack tried not to apologize. People seemed to want you to apologize for no reason in the great city. Jack was determined not to get caught up in that nonsense, those ubiquitous land mines for neophyted visitors.

A waitress marched in without greeting, wearing a linen doily hairpinned atop her head. She clattered down the latticed walkway into the kitchen, and reappeared with order pad and sponge in hand after shedding her coat. The owner did not greet her but did frown silent lips in glancing up to find 7:06 AM registered on the wall clock.

Jack ordered the special and sipped his coffee. The owner, glum over Jack knowing neither Agnes Schweepner or Ernie Trawick, made his way around the double horseshoe of counter redistributing wet dust with his sponge, and began to chat with two new customers who had shuffled in to take up lodging on stools as far from Jack and from each other as was geometrically possible.

One, a dumpy man in an armor of clashing sweaters warmed his hands in a steeple of prayer above his smoking coffee; the other, a blubbery woman toting a shopping bag with a greasy, floppy handle, wheezed through a total inspection of her upholstered purse, grunting periodically under the weight of her soiled parka which was trimmed at the collar with some dead animal.

Jack ate ravenously. The food is always excellent in the great city. The plays and shows are excellent. The museums are excellent. It's just that the people, well . . .

Rising to leave, Jack patted his tummy. The waitress, now serving four or five new customers, handed the order slip to her boss. He tallied it while moving around the horseshoe and met Jack at the register, lamenting the unfortunate World Series game loss to the Beantowners the night before.

$4.95 he rung on the register.

"I asked for the special," Jack said.

"The special?," repeated the owner. His thespian act was an abbreviated one act flop in New Haven.

"Outside on the glass," motioned Jack.

"Oh! that. Hell, I didn't know it was still on."

He rang up the right amount, scowling. He was extremely sorry now that Jack didn't know Agnes Schweepner or Ernie Trawick.

Jack took the liberty at the coffee shop entrance of shooting a libation-of-the-spirit grin back to the owner, that pyrrhic victory look of "not this time, buddy," that utter satisfaction which, once in a while, reminds one that indeed life can be worthwhile. The owner read it well, and lobbed his own expression back — you got me this time, but there will be others.

Jack slunk back to the hotel, buying a Sunday newspaper he could devour all morning long propped up in bed. In the narrow lobby, the cage attendant who had gleamed white teeth at Jack when they had arrived two days earlier, was at the verbal throat of a ruffian.

"Wake him up."

"He's asleep."

"Wake him up."

"He's asleep."

"I don't care, wake him up."

"He's asleep. I will not wake."

"I said wake him up."

"I call police."

Jack nodded for his key, stretching his arm around the cage as gingerly as one would feed peanuts to a growling zoo animal. Then he escaped lightly to the stairwell next to the tiny elevator, glancing all about him on the slick carpet expecting to find a heap of dead bodies littered about. He took the steps, advancing on the liquid asphalt swimming on the roof. He wasn't about to have the world end with him in that postage stamp elevator. His son slept on despite Jack's key clunking in the lock as loud as a time card stamped in a riveting factory clock.

The home team lost the first two games of the World Series and the biggest city in the land took the affront personally. In newspaper kiosks, midnight coffee shoppes, lobbies of hotels, and everywhere along the millipedal trample on the crowded sidewalks, staunch baseball devotees cursed their luck.

The two games were spectacular nevertheless — surely as exciting as any extravaganza staged millennia ago at the Roman Circus Maximus or Coliseum. The bundled crowds roared at foul tips and at weak pop flies and gasped in unison at trickling, puny grounders. They stood at the slightest provocation.

Heartened by the memory of his marvelous Saturday morning at the elbow of the Samaritan judge, Jack was again in high spirits when he and his son parted at their hotel. His son bussed across the other well-known river for his "no frills" flight back to college from the airport in the neighboring state. Jack lugged his suitcase downstairs for the short jaunt up the incline of pavement to a bus, which would hiss and belch him across a river of his own, to his flight at the airport where he had landed three days earlier.

Jack rested his suitcase on the pavement at the corner. It was heavy. His hand tingled with numbness. He decided to indulge himself with the debatable luxury of one last taxi ride. He was smartly dressed in a herring-boned, gray jacket and matching sweater and slacks, and easily could have passed for some corporate insider exiting the city, save for a necktie which did not, this morning, adorn his throat.

After he telegraphed his raised signal of hand, a yellow steed of commerce snorted to the curb. Jack slid his suitcase across the dusty backseat, and followed with his rump in beside it. Immediately, he received the distinct impression again from the plexiglass window separating the two seats that he was being whisked away to a glary police lineup, as a prime suspect in some ghastly crime.

"Just up the road a piece, kind sir — the bus stop by the terminal," Jack said, ladling renewed milk of human kindness for another go at sane relations with a cab driver, still awash with the warm glow of Saturday morning passed.

"What?," growled the cabby, mouthing his harsh pronoun bluntly, around a wet cigar clenched by yellowing teeth.

Perspiration pooled at the small of Jack's back and his neck was tossed into a microwave oven.

"Yes, just up there." Jack pointed ahead, in the direction of the great building straddling the fashionable street.

"C'mon, get serious."

"I am serious."

Silence reigned.

Jack sat quietly, as one does in Sunday church just after the organ stops, moments before the real service is to begin. He surveyed his mobile prison. The driver caught a picket of red lights on the short blocks, agitating further his distinct annoyance with his dumb luck capture of this undersized fare.

A makeshift cardboard placard, faded and stained, taped to the sliding interior window, scrawled crudely with the words, *THIS DRIVER MAKES NO CHANGE,* affronted the retinas in Jack's eyes. A sharp yellow pencil, lodged above the driver's right ear, pointed its honed tip to the rear seat.

Jack scooted a few inches to his right, still tethering his suitcase with one protective hand, fearful that the pencil was a lethal dart for undertippers, with its black graphite possibly dipped in poisonous, blowgun curare paste. The wet cigar swam around the driver's sulking mouth. It made a total Magellan circle about his smacking lips, but he remained silent as a grave, up the braking cavalcade of red traffic lights.

"I guess you were expecting a nice easy fare to one of the airports, against the grain of morning traffic coming in, seeing me with the suitcase?", ventured Jack. He had been to Brooklyn on Saturday. He now brandished little rancor in his heart over shoddy treatment. He felt he could calm Lucifer himself.

"Sumphin' like that," mumbled the cabby, hunching his soiled shoulders further over the steering wheel.

For half a block they parried unspokenly, only their brains spoke, privately to each. Jack smiled at an old adage he dredged up. 'Whoever speaks first, loses.' Jack risked a wound. He could afford the vulnerability. He had experienced his mountain-top Saturday.

"Why don't you erect a sign that says, *I WILL TREAT YOU LIKE A HUMAN BEING IF I REALLY LIKE THE FARE YOU GIVE ME.*'" Jack was not sarcastic, just a trifle weary with a tidy wrapper of matter-of-factness draped about his statement. He knew he would be punished anyhow, so why not be bold and rout out doormatitis with assertiveness, a medicinal tonic, personally administered, which would at least make him feel better.

His fate was stamped with a king's seal. The entire neck of the cabby disappeared within his carapace of sweatered shoulders. He smoldered like a stirred volcano. His wet cigar galloped about his mouth. Gallows for Jack were hammered up somehwere in the distance. Jack leaned back in his seat, a doomed man but one who was mentally purged. He wondered what ploy the driver would use as sharp guillotine against his comment.

The cabby careened to a screeching halt well across the street from the bus stop, leaving Jack a nasty, unnecessary intersection crossing amid a flotsam sea of early morning vendors dashing about in grinding trucks.

"Ah!", breathed Jack, smiling. "That one — the old, 'I can't get closer trick.'"

Jack opened his door at the curb, after crawling up and over his suitcase, and drew a single Abraham Lincoln bill from his jacket pocket. He held it aloft conspicously, like a carrot in the hand of a morning handler in front of a frisky colt. The cabby eyed the bill hungrily, knowing change was not his to make on the paltry $1.80 fare. The placard in his cab had decreed that no change need be made. He was practically home free with the Lincoln five-spot.

Jack dangled the bill just out of reach. The cabby beaded his eyes, and salivated his drooping cigar until he choked.

"Have you ever been to a quaint cranberry festival? Have you ever walked the Promenade, picturing how the river might have appeared at night from there to Thomas Wolfe? Have you ever stood at the wooden door of the great church where a fiery preacher boomed powerful sermons?"

Jack waited for an answer. None formed. Only a scowl blackly hooded the cab.

"You can't defeat me. There are fine people here. I encountered one of them only last Saturday," Jack leaned in for a final thrust, wrestling his bulky suitcase to the sidewalk. He handed across the money.

"Wiseguy," daggered the cabby, pouncing the bill into a shirt pocket. His cigar and pencil poised as sharp arrows in his edgy arsenal of weaponry.

His meter clattered noisily as he clubbed it back to a line of zeroes for the next fare and he thundered out again upstream, into the swim of things among the trucks and the army of kindred yellow beetles swarming on the avenue.

ABOUT THE AUTHOR

Born in upstate New York, Ed L'Heureux grew up in Central Florida, and has spent his adult life there. He attended schools in Winter Park, Florida, graduated from Stetson University in Deland, Florida, and also studied law at the University of Florida and Stetson University.

Over the past twenty years, he has pursued careers in the securities industry as a stockbroker, in commercial real estate development, and in the field of insurance. Currently, he operates his own insurance agency in Central Florida and has done so for the past eleven years.

Writing has always been one of his favorite pastimes, with greater emphasis, avocationally, placed with the endeavor in recent years. After a number of magazine feature articles to his credit, Mr. L'Heureux published his first collection of short stories, *THE DOLLAR COLLAR* in 1986. This work, *THE CLAY OF VASES,* is his second collection of short stories. His first novel is completed and slated for release in 1988.

He lives in Winter Springs, Florida, with his wife, Laura, and his two children, Scott and Stacey.

THE CLAY OF VASES AND OTHER STORIES

Order Form for THE CLAY OF VASES

Please send _____ copies of THE CLAY OF VASES to:

Name _____

Address _____

_____

_____

_____

Enclosed is my check for

Price: $6.95 plus $1.00 shipping (Florida residents add 5%
sales tax)

Kindly   Ed L'Heureux
Send order forms and   P.O. Box 3633
make checks payable to: Winter Springs, FL 32708

THE CLAY OF VASES AND OTHER STORIES

Order Form for THE CLAY OF VASES

Please send _____ copies of THE CLAY OF VASES to:

Name _____

Address _____

_____

_____

_____

Enclosed is my check for

Price: $6.95 plus $1.00 shipping (Florida residents add 5%
sales tax)

Kindly	Ed L'Heureux
Send order forms and	P.O. Box 3633
make checks payable to:	Winter Springs, FL 32708

THE CLAY OF VASES AND OTHER STORIES

Order Form for THE CLAY OF VASES

Please send _____ copies of THE CLAY OF VASES to:

Name _____

Address _____

_____

_____

_____

Enclosed is my check for

Price: $6.95 plus $1.00 shipping (Florida residents add 5%
sales tax)

Kindly	Ed L'Heureux
Send order forms and	P.O. Box 3633
make checks payable to:	Winter Springs, FL 32708

THE CLAY OF VASES AND OTHER STORIES

Order Form for THE CLAY OF VASES

Please send _____ copies of THE CLAY OF VASES to:

Name _____

Address _____

_____

_____

_____

Enclosed is my check for

Price: $6.95 plus $1.00 shipping (Florida residents add 5% sales tax)

Kindly   Ed L'Heureux
Send order forms and   P.O. Box 3633
make checks payable to: Winter Springs, FL 32708